W9-CXL-245

DEMIGODS ACADEMY

YEAR ONE

ELISA S. AMORE
KIERA LEGEND

Amore publishing

Copyright © 2019 by Amore Publishing

All rights reserved.

No part of this book may be reproduced in any form or by any electronic or mechanical means, including information storage and retrieval systems, without written permission from the author, except for the use of brief quotations in a book review.

.

To Giuseppe Amore who got the idea to fill the academy with Gods and Demigods.

DEMIGODS ACADEMY

CHAPTER ONE

MELANY

*T*here were more than one hundred people at Callie's eighteenth birthday party milling about in the northwest great room, drinking from champagne flutes and eating pickled fig and ricotta canapés passed out by uniformed waiters and waitresses. They were friends from her prestigious private prep school, their parents, and members of her big Greek family. I stood among them, although I didn't belong to any of those groups. To my face, Callie would definitely call me a friend, sister even, as I'd lived in close proximity to her for the past five years, but I knew behind my back she whispered to her parents, her friends, even the staff who worked in the big house about how I didn't truly belong.

And the sad thing was she wouldn't be wrong.

I took a sip of champagne, as I leaned against the white railing of the veranda, and stared out over the grounds of the Demos Estate. It was lit up by solar garden lamps lining the cobblestone pathways and winding around the various stone statues guarding the back entrance to the house, as well as out front near the drive. It was always beautiful here at night. I'd often go for long, secret walks through the garden after midnight, my adopted mother, Sophia, and the rest of the Demos household none the wiser. Well, the gardener, Bishop, knew of my late night outings, as he'd caught me a time or two sprinting through the grass and leaping over the stone benches peppered throughout—my own private obstacle course. But he'd never rat me out. We had an understanding. He wouldn't snitch on me about my clandestine nighttime adventures, and I wouldn't tell anyone he smoked weed behind the garden shed with Rachel, who was one of the cooking staff.

"What are you doing out here?" Callie joined me at the railing, the sleeves of her elegant blue gown draping over the white wood. She looked like a queen. Her hair was wrapped in a complicated braid around her head, like the Greek Goddesses wore theirs. She even wore a tiny diamond-encrusted tiara for the occasion.

"You know, the usual. Hiding out. Keeping away from Cousin Leo's grabby hands." I made the motion to tweak one of Callie's boobs.

She laughed and slapped my hand away. "I know,

he's terrible. He grabbed Kate's ass earlier."

I took another sip of champagne, feeling aware I wasn't even close to looking as beautiful and elegant as Callie did. I hadn't worn a fancy gown, instead opting for a classic black long-sleeved cape jumpsuit. It wasn't mine; Callie loaned it to me. I could never afford something like that. I also suspected it was chosen for me, so it would cover the tattoos on my arms and legs. Her parents were very traditional and uptight. They only put up with me because I was the daughter of their most trusted housekeeper.

"It's time to come in now." Callie turned and gestured to the large room bustling with people in tuxes and gowns beyond the open terrace doors, the din of conversation buzzing annoyingly in my ears. "I'm going to be opening my Shadowbox soon. You want to be there when I do."

"Sure. I'll be right in. Give me a minute."

"You better be. You won't want to miss seeing me get my invitation to the Gods' Army."

I smirked. "You know that's a million in one shot."

Her eyes narrowed into slits. "I didn't waste my life worshipping at the temples for nothing."

Callie walked back into the party. Her feet didn't appear like they touched the floor; her gown was so long it dragged on the immaculate, white-tiled floor. She seemed to float she was so graceful. Often people compared her to the Goddess Aphrodite—long, golden blonde hair, perfect, symmetrical facial features, glacial blue eyes, and the nose of an aristocrat. I thought she also possessed some of the Goddess's character traits as well: vain, sly, and just a little bit diabolical.

Well, maybe not diabolical. People often saved that word to describe me. Not that I blamed them. My midnight blue hair, tattoos, piercings, and snarly attitude were a bit out of place in the upper class neighborhood of Pecunia, where the families were mostly Greek and devout to the Gods. It wasn't like I didn't believe in the Gods—I sort of had faith. I just didn't worship them like everyone else did. They'd done nothing for me in my life. In my opinion, they didn't deserve my patronage.

Every Thursday, the Demos family went to the Temple of Zeus with their offerings of wine, which they made here on the estate, and lamb sausage, which a butcher in the neighborhood made especially for religious ceremonies, and laid them at the stone feet of the statue of Zeus. Then they spent the day with the other worshippers, drinking and eating. I'd gone once with them years ago, but found the whole practice ridiculous and uncomfortable.

To me, the whole thing was just a story passed down from generation to generation, going on more than a hundred years now. A story we all grew up listening to and reading about in our children's books about the resurgence of the Gods during the New Dawn. I'd read about the 1906 and 1908 earthquakes that killed hundreds of thousands of people, supposedly caused by the escape of a Titan from their prison, and how the Gods fought him and returned him to

Tartarus. Worshipping the Gods ensured no other Titan would escape. And the Shadowboxes delivered to every child turning eighteen was a gift from the Gods in return for that servitude. Ninety-nine percent of the boxes contained a simple birthday message, but there was that one percent that held a special invitation to join the demigods academy to train to be a soldier of the Gods.

I thought most of it was just a load of crap. I mean, the Gods' Army? That couldn't possibly be true. Where was this army? Who was part of it? No one in more than a hundred years had seen any evidence of it. It was just another way for companies to make a buck. The amount of Blessed Day birthday supplies designed and sold to the devout was ridiculous. Especially since the chances of someone being invited to join the Gods' Army was miniscule—if it was even real. I'd never known anyone to be chosen. For me, it was just as much a myth as the Gods themselves.

When I joined the others back in the party, the crowd had formed a semi-circle around Callie, while she stood near the baby grand piano at the front of the spacious room. Her parents stood beside her; her mother beamed with pride. Her father appeared stoic. In fact in all the years I'd lived on the estate, I didn't think I'd ever seen Mr. Demos smile. Or it could've been he never smiled at or around me.

I spotted a few of Callie's friends, who I despised, standing near her at the front. Her best friend, Ashley, looked in thrall with the festivities. On the other hand,

Tyler appeared bored to tears. When our gazes locked, he gave me a giant, fake smile then lifted his hand and flipped me the middle finger.

I returned the gesture just as the lights flashed off, and a huge birthday cake was wheeled in on a serving table by two of the cooking staff. Someone in the back started singing Happy Birthday, and then it gained momentum through the crowd as the cake, with its eighteen tall, flickering candles, got closer to the birthday girl.

Callie plastered a fabricated smile on her face, as her guests' song reached a high-pitched fervor. Then she blew out the candles and everyone clapped. I knew what her wish would be: an invitation to the mystical Gods' Army. Knowing Callie, she'd probably get it, as she received everything she wanted.

As the cake was wheeled away to be surgically cut into the perfect triangle-shaped pieces, a triumphant horn blew from outside. A murmur rippled through the crowd. The Shadowbox had arrived.

As everyone held their breath in anticipation of the presentation of the famed metal box, I swallowed down my resentment. I hated all this pomp and ceremony. It was a bitter reminder that on my eighteenth birthday, I hadn't received a Shadowbox. Although the magic box was supposed to be delivered to every child across the world on their eighteenth birthday, that momentous, blessed event had missed me entirely. And I wasn't sure why.

A hush fell over the congregation, as a dignitary of

the Gods dressed in a traditional Greek white robe carried the metal box in on a clay platter. Fig leaves were embroidered along the edges. I craned my neck and jostled for position with others to get a better view of the box as it made its way to the front of the room.

Even during my time at the orphanage, I'd heard about the boxes—no kid grew up without hearing about them—but the reality of one paled in comparison to any elaborate story. Maybe they weren't the myths I'd thought them to be. But just because the Shadowboxes were real, didn't mean the rest of it was.

The Shadowbox was breathtaking. Constructed from bronze and inlaid with gold and silver, it seemed to glow with its own radiance. Beside me, someone gasped as the dignitary stopped in front of Callie, presenting her with the gift.

Now that it was closer, I could see the motifs engraved with painstaking detail into the metal: symbols of the Gods. The lightning bolt of Zeus, the star of Hera, the rose of Aphrodite, the wolf of Ares. I could see those plain as day. I imagined on the other side would be the moon of Artemis and the sun of Apollo, along with another six symbols to round out the pantheon.

Callie looked at her mother and father to get their permission to open the box. They both nodded. Before she could open it though, she needed to give her thanks to the Gods. It was tradition.

"I thank Thee, mighty Gods. To those who dwell in Olympus, apart from man yet always a part of our lives. To those who dwell in city, forest, stream, river, sky, and ocean and guard all realms, I thank Thee for your blessings and hope to be worthy of the call." Her voice cracked as she spoke, and I almost felt sorry for her. Almost.

Slowly, she reached for the box. When she picked it up, many in the audience gasped. I wasn't sure what they were expecting; maybe for light to shoot out of it, but that wasn't what happened. It might've been Callie had been expecting that as well, because her face fell a little with disappointment.

Lifting the lid, she peered inside. Her hand gave a slight tremble as she reached inside and drew out the tiny rolled-up scroll fastened with a gold ribbon. I could see her throat working as she swallowed nervously while she untied the ribbon and unfurled the weathered, yellowing parchment.

As Callie read the message written on the scroll, her cheeks reddened. Obviously, she didn't receive the message she'd been expecting.

"What does it say, darling?" Her mother craned her long neck trying to read over her daughter's arm.

Callie nudged her mother away as she threw the box to the ground and ran out of the room. Some of the guests murmured at Callie's shocking behavior. Frankly, it didn't surprise me in the least. Smiling, Mrs. Demos nodded to the five-piece band set up in the corner, and music filled the room. She gestured to the partygoers.

"Let's get on the dance floor everyone. This is a

party, for Dionysus's sake!'"

She grabbed my arm, pulling me close. "Go find Callie and tell her to get her butt back in here and make her apologies. She doesn't want to offend the Gods." She gestured to the box on the ground near her feet. "Take that with you."

I snatched it up, shocked to feel an instant tingle on my fingers. I thought the metal would feel cool to the touch, but there was a heat radiating from it enveloping my fingers and creeping up my hands to my wrists.

I found Callie out on the terrace smoking. She didn't look at me as I stepped up beside her.

"Are you okay?"

She kept puffing. "I can't believe after all the offerings we've made to the temples, and all the charity work my parents do…" She shook her head. "And I get a stupid birthday blessing and not an invitation to the academy."

"Yeah, that totally sucks." I wanted to roll my eyes at her entitled behavior, but didn't want to invoke her rage.

She whipped around to glare at me. "I'm the perfect candidate. I'm everything they need at the academy. I would have been one of their best soldiers."

"Your mother told me to tell you to come back inside and apologize to your guests." I held the Shadowbox out to her. "Here's your box back."

She slapped it away, and I nearly dropped it. "I don't want it. You can fucking burn it for all I care. I don't ever want to see it again!"

She ground out her cigarette on the railing and then stormed back into the house. I watched her leave, feeling anger welling inside me. Callie acted like a spoiled child, which I supposed she was. And one of the cleaning staff was going to get in trouble over the damage she just did to the wooden railing. If it ended up being Sophia, I was most definitely going to say something.

Tired of the theatrics of the party, I snuck out of the house with the box and crossed the garden to the small cottage on the edge of the estate where I lived with Sophia. Screw Callie. I wasn't going to burn the box. If anything, I could hock it and probably get thousands for it.

Careful not to wake Sophia, who was likely already asleep in bed, as she'd left the party early after working hard for three days to plan the celebration, I crept through the house to my small bedroom.

"You don't have to creep, I'm not sleeping."

Hiding the Shadowbox behind my back, I turned toward the small living room to see Sophia sitting in her chair near the window with knitting needles in her hands, and a ball of red wool in her lap.

"Why are you in the dark knitting?" I smiled at her.

"It relaxes me. There's too much going on in my head to go to sleep."

"Did you hear about Callie?"

She clucked her tongue. "Yes, I heard. Spoiled girl. Some days I don't know how Mrs. Demos puts up with her."

She gestured to the floor by her feet where I usually liked to sit and listen to her tell stories about her and my parents when they were children. "Come sit with me. Tell me everything you got up to today. Did you get a piece of cake? I heard it was delicious."

"No, I didn't get a piece. Not surprising with all the commotion going on." I feigned a yawn. "I'm going to go to bed. It's been a long night."

"Okay, my darling. Have sweet dreams."

"Sweet dreams." I took a few steps backward, then whipped around with the box so I could duck into my room without her seeing it.

I quickly got out of the jumpsuit, careful not to get it dirty, and put on a pair of sweatpants and an old tank top that had several holes in it from wear and tear over the years. Money was tight for us, so I didn't spend it frivolously on clothing that didn't matter.

Once I was dressed comfortably, I sat cross-legged on the bed and held the box. Again, a strange heat emanated from it and rushed up my hands. Feeling unsettled, I set the box down in front of me. I'd been right about the symbols etched into the metal. There were definitely twelve of them, representing each powerful being.

As I studied the craftsmanship, I was in awe. I'd never seen anything as intricate and beautiful before in my life. With careful hands, I lifted the lid on the box, expecting it to be empty, as Callie had already taken out the scroll and her message from the Gods.

But it wasn't empty. Another small, rolled-up scroll nestled inside, white against the purple velvet.

Confusion crinkled my brow. Callie must've missed this scroll in her haste. She had been overly anxious, and there were so many people crowded around watching; she must've plucked one scroll out and totally missed the other.

I reached in and took it out. The second I touched the paper my fingers tingled. I knew I should just put the scroll back inside and return the box to Callie, but something told me to open and read it. So, I did.

I pulled the ribbon off and unrolled the parchment.

Congratulations, recruit! You've been invited to the Gods' Army.

My heart picked up, revving like a motorcycle in my chest. An electrical shock went through my fingers, and I dropped the scroll. The paper fluttered in the air for a few seconds then landed gracefully onto my blanket.

I couldn't believe it. Callie missed this in her spoiled temper tantrum. The proper and moral thing to do was to roll the message back up, place it in the Shadowbox, and return it to Callie, so she could go to the demigods academy and train to be a righteous soldier for the Gods. But I didn't want to.

Callie had everything: loving parents, a good home,

lots of money and possessions, friends. And she didn't appreciate any of it, not one morsel. She always complained to me about not having enough, or her parents not letting her run off to the Cayman Islands in the middle of a school term. She complained about not being pretty enough, or thin enough, gorging on caviar and macarons, while three neighborhoods over, people were homeless and starving.

A thought crossed my mind. What if I kept it for myself? No one would know. Callie already thought the Gods had rejected her, commanding me to destroy the beautiful Shadowbox. She'd never know. If the academy really existed, maybe it would give me true purpose—something I'd never been able to find.

For the last eighteen years, I'd felt lost, like a ship without an anchor, being tossed around in a storm. I'd been an outcast my entire life, not knowing my parents, wondering why they'd left me, always feeling like I was worthless. And now, I could finally become someone who had worth and direction.

It was a once-in-a-lifetime-chance, and it required a hard decision.

I stared down at the box, my heart and my head at war. I had done really bad things in my life but stealing Callie's opportunity to attend the Gods' Academy? It was going to be the worst.

I knew it was wrong, but my heart longed to find my place in the world. Was it at the academy? I couldn't know… but I had to find out.

CHAPTER TWO

MELANY

I picked up the parchment lying on my bed and flipped it around, looking for the rest. Rumor was that inside the box, along with the invitation to the academy, would be instructions on how to get to the famed but secret institution and the date and time. I didn't see any of those things scrawled on the paper.

Lifting the box, I peered inside it again, paying particular attention to any clever hiding spot for another scroll. I ran my fingers along the smooth edges and planes to find nothing. But when I touched the velvet inlay on the bottom, a tiny bit of the corner curled up. Maybe there was something underneath.

I gripped the velvet between my fingers and tore it away. It didn't come easily, and I had to remove it in strips. When it was gone, I squinted into the box and saw an inscription etched into the metal on the bottom. I held the box up to my lamp and read the words out loud.

"To reveal the secrets of the academy, you must use the thing that has no legs but dances, has no lungs but breathes, and has no life to live or die, but does all three."

A riddle. *Perfect.* I groaned.

It couldn't be too hard, or none of the recruits would make it to the designated time and place, but I supposed that was the point, as they'd only want the best of the best. I read it over again, trying to put the pieces together.

I rose from my bed and paced a little. I did all my best thinking while moving around. What could dance, breathe, and live or die? Humans, but that wasn't it, as we had legs and lungs and had a life. It couldn't be an animal because the same parameters existed. As I marched around my room, my gaze kept going back to the Shadowbox. Every now and then, it would flash from a direct beam of light reflecting off the metal as I moved around it. I thought about how it felt in my hands; the wave of heat that rushed over my skin. Halting, I picked up the box again and studied the symbols of the Gods etched on the exterior.

Zeus – lightning.
Hera – star.

Aphrodite – rose.
Ares – wolf.
Apollo – sun.
Artemis – moon.

I flipped it around and looked at the other six, something irritating my mind like a piece of a popcorn kernel stuck in my teeth.

Poseidon – trident.
Dionysus – chalice.
Hephaistos – fire.
Athena – owl.
Demeter – cornucopia.
Hermes – snake.

Frowning, I brushed my fingers over the box, feeling the metal. Again, heat enveloped my fingers. It was as if I'd set my hand over a burner on a stove. The craftsmanship of the metalwork was beyond anything earthly. It had to have been designed by one of the Gods. Heat, metal…

Fire.

That had to be it. Flames in a fire appeared like they were dancing, fire needed oxygen, like lungs did, to burn, and fire could be snuffed out, the flames dying. That had to be the answer. There was only one way to find out.

Since I didn't have a fireplace to make a fire in, I gathered all the pillar candles I had in my room, set them in a cluster, and lit them. Then I held the Shadowbox up over the tiny individual flames, hoping I wasn't making a fool out of myself in thinking how clever I was.

I held the box over the candles for ten minutes at least before I could feel a temperature difference in the metal. After another few minutes, it started to become difficult to hold, as my fingers burned. Wincing at the sharp pain, I didn't know how much longer I could keep the box over the flames.

Reaching my threshold, I was about to drop it when thin curls of black smoke rippled out from inside the box. The vapors snaked around in the air, animated, as if blown by an unseen wind. I looked to my window to see if it was open; it wasn't. It was closed tight. At first, I thought the smoke nothing more than a result of melting metal, but then the tendrils started to make words and numbers in the air.

Cala.

3 a.m.

Pier…

I leaned forward, my breath hitching in my throat, as a number formed. But I couldn't decipher if it was a nine or a six. It looped around, set into a spin by either the unseen wind or my frantic breathing. It looked like a six, then a nine, then it stayed as a six. Then after it had all formed in front of me, as if someone had been writing it in the air with a quill and ink... it vanished.

The flames on the candles flared. I dropped the box, as my fingers couldn't hold it any longer. I glanced down at my hands; the tips of my fingers were red, and a few tiny blisters had formed. It didn't matter, as I had my information.

Cala was the small town near the bay. There was a large dock there; Sophia had taken me there once to watch the huge cruise ships come in. I didn't know how many piers were there, but I only had to find the one— pier six. And it had to be at three a.m. I grabbed my cell phone and looked at the time. It was eleven. I had four hours to get to the right spot to find the academy.

It didn't give me much time to reconsider my decision or to think about the consequences of it, either. If I was going to go, it had to be now.

I jumped to my feet, went into my closet, and grabbed an old ratty duffle bag that I'd had since being in the orphanage. I opened dresser drawers and grabbed whatever I could—underwear, bras, socks, jeans, a couple of T-shirts—and stuffed them inside the bag. On top of that, I settled in the Shadowbox. I imagined I would need it as some sort of proof that I belonged.

After zipping up the bag, I put on my old weathered leather jacket, my combat boots, slid my phone in a pocket, and then peered out. Sophia wasn't in the living room and her bedroom was closed, so she'd obviously gone to bed. After stepping out from my bedroom, I stopped in front of Sophia's closed door. I wanted to leave her a note to let her know where I'd gone, but I knew that would confess what I'd done. No one could know that I'd stolen the invitation. Instead, I quietly opened her door and crept in.

My heart filled when I looked down at her, sleeping so soundly, her face relaxed and devoid of all the worry lines I knew I'd carved on her skin over the years. Leaning down, I pressed a kiss to her forehead and whispered, "I love you."

Fighting back tears, I left the cottage and crept silently across the garden, keeping to the dark shadows, until I reached the driveway. As far as I knew, there weren't any buses that came to this neighborhood, nor would any be running this late, anyway, so I needed a way to get to Cala, which was at least ninety miles away from Pecunia. I had only three and a half hours to get there on time. On foot, I'd never make it.

I heard voices nearby. It had to be party guests leaving. For a brief second, I considered hitching a ride with one of them, but they would definitely inform Callie. I couldn't have that. I needed to leave here undetected, at least until sunrise. In the morning, they could all think what they wanted. Most likely that I'd run away. According to them, I was that type of girl. Sophia wouldn't think it though, she'd worry that something nefarious had happened to me, or that I had a good reason to leave. It broke my heart to put her through the anguish of not knowing, but I had to do it.

. . .

Headlights swept over the spot of pavement I stood in, and I jumped back, breath hitching, into the shadows, so I wouldn't be seen. When I turned, I spotted a street motorcycle parked in the corner away from all the other vehicles. That had not been valet parked.

A smile crept over my face, and I sent up a small thanks to the Gods, although I knew they couldn't give a shit and weren't likely paying any attention to what I was doing. I was insignificant.

Ten minutes later, I raced down the driveway of the Demos Estate, thankful of the illegal skills I'd learned during my time in and out of foster homes. I turned left onto the main road and roared out of Pecunia. Although I was excited to have my past in the rear view mirror, I felt guilty for leaving Sophia. I hoped over time she'd understand why I left.

My heart raced as fast as the bike as I drove toward the coast. I couldn't believe what I was doing. I prayed it would work. I needed it to work. If it didn't and I was booted out before I could even begin, I wasn't sure I'd return to Pecunia. Maybe it would be a sign to just keep on going until the road ended, and I could have a new start.

I thought about that all the way to Cala.

It didn't take me long to find the dock, as the touristy town was fairly small, and all I needed to do was follow the sounds of the ocean. I parked the bike at the main boathouse and then climbed over the chain link fence.

As I made my way to pier six, the silence surprised me. Where were all the other recruits? Surely, I wasn't the only one who figured out the riddle and was able to get here. The rumors were that every four years the Gods recruited thirty-six teenagers to train in the army. I'm not sure why that particular number, but knowing the Gods, it likely had some significance. So, where was everybody?

I found pier six easily enough, despite the lack of overhead lights. As I walked out to the edge, the darkness smothering me with each step, an eerie quiet settled over everything. All I could hear was the soft lapping of the water at the metal posts holding the pier up and my heart thundering in my chest.

I gazed out over the rolling ocean and thought, now what? Did I need to wait for a boat or something? But that seemed almost too easy for the Gods. Knowing them, the way into the academy would be complicated and dangerous. It was like Jason was just given the Golden Fleece; he had to complete three very complicated trials wrought with danger at every turn.

I wondered if I would get a chance to meet Jason at the academy and ask him how he escaped smashing onto the rocks when a school of sirens attacked the ship he'd been on. All my thoughts about ships and sirens made me speculate the entrance to the academy was going to be underwater.

Squinting, I looked out over the water and spotted a

buoy floating about a hundred meters away. Every few seconds, it lit up. That was where I needed to go. Strapping my duffel to my back, I took in some deep breaths, wondering if I was really going to do this.

"One, two, three." I dove into the water.

I swam down into the darkness, expecting something to happen. A portal. A door. I'd even take a submarine at this point. But there was nothing but seaweed and the soul-sucking black of deep water. Lungs bursting, I started upwards, my arms aching with fatigue by the time I broke the surface. I sputtered out water and circled around toward the pier.

And that's when I heard the very male sounds of laughter and spotted the outline of someone on the end of the pier watching me. I didn't have to see him to know he was getting a right kick out of seeing me floundering around like a guppy.

"Little late for a midnight swim, don't you think?"

I swam to the pier. The closer I got, the more I could make out the person's features. He was definitely male, and young, my age I thought, square jaw, sharp cheekbones, golden waves swept back to frame striking blue eyes, and to my misfortune, he was exactly the type of guy I'd swoon over.

I reached up and grabbed the edge of the wooden dock so I could heft myself out of the water. He took a step forward, and I thought for sure he was going to crush my fingers under the thick tread of his combat boots, especially when he grinned down at me.

CHAPTER THREE

MELANY

I was about to drop back into the water to avoid having my fingers crushed when he crouched and grabbed hold of my arms, lugging me up onto the pier. I rolled onto my back, dragging hair out my face, and blinked up at him, unsure if he was friend or foe.

"You're on the wrong pier." He nodded toward the other piers, and I spotted several other teenagers my age making their way down the main dock, backpacks slung over their shoulders, or firmly affixed to their backs.

I sat up, trying to keep some of my dignity intact, although I suspected it was much too late for that considering I was sitting here sopping wet, my hair looking like blue seaweed, and I could just imagine my dark makeup had run down my cheeks. The gorgeous stranger probably thought I looked like some deranged raccoon.

"Maybe I just wanted to go swimming." I wiped at my face with the sleeve of my jacket, which didn't do much of anything since it was wet, too.

"Right." He offered his hand to help me to my feet, but I ignored it and stood my own. He lowered his hand, shaking his head a little. "It's pier nine, in case you're wondering. You must've misread the smoke." Picking up his pack, he walked away, joining the swarm of other people.

Before following him, I waited for a few minutes. I didn't want to seem eager or that he'd just saved me from a huge mistake, although, he totally did. I got in line with the others moving down the ramp to pier nine. There had to have been at least thirty people, maybe more, gathered on the dock.

No one was really talking to each other, except for my mysterious savior. He was near the front of the pack, chatting it up with another guy and a pretty girl with long, dark hair. She giggled a lot and kept touching his arm. I hated her on principle, alone.

I took out my phone, which of course was now wet, but I'd wrapped it in plastic before I left, so it wasn't completely damaged. The time said it was 2:55 a.m. We were all cutting it close. I wondered what everyone was waiting for. Maybe I had got it wrong, and there really was a boat coming for us, which would mean I made an even bigger fool out of myself then I needed to.

The guy standing next to me frowned. "Are you wet?"

"Yes. Do you have a problem with that?"

He shook his head. "Nope. Each to their own, I say." He said it with such conviction that I smiled. He returned my smile then it faded a bit. "Are you scared?"

"Hell no." I peered at him, taking in his lanky frame and perfectly coifed jet-black hair. "Are you?"

He scuffed his converse sneaker on the dock. "Nah, I'm ready for the academy."

Except he didn't look all that ready. In fact, none of the people on the dock looked ready. Except for maybe mystery guy. He seemed ready for anything; he had that kind of confidence about him.

Almost everyone flinched when twenty-some alarms sounded on twenty-some cell phones. It was three o'clock. One by one, people leapt off the pier and into the water. It was more like a mass exodus than single file. When I got to the edge, I dove in as well.

This time, I knew where to go. I just followed the swimmer in front of me, as we all dove down. It was dark and murky, extremely difficult to see anything in any direction. But then up ahead, I spied a soft white glow. Everyone's course adjusted, and they swam toward the light.

The closer I got to the light, I saw that it was a blue-white cylinder hovering in the middle of the vast dark ocean like a giant glowing worm. It was a portal. This was how we were all going to get to the academy.

Each person who reached the portal ahead of me breached the barrier and was swept up into it. It looked like they were being sucked up through a large, white straw. Maybe one of the Titans was having a delicious cool glass of water, and we were the dirt specks getting drunk along the way.

As I got nearer, my heart hammered in my throat and my lungs burned. I didn't know how much longer I could hold my breath. Slowly, I reached out to the portal. My fingers pushed through the barrier, and I could feel the suction on my hand. If I weren't careful, my fingers would be ripped off from the force.

Here goes nothing.

I kicked my legs harder, propelling myself forward, and was instantly engulfed by the whirlpool. I hurtled along inside the portal, my body spinning around and around. It was hard to focus on anything, as I was spun like cotton candy.

The guy who'd been standing beside me did a couple of somersaults in the water as he hurtled by me, a huge smile on his face. While I watched him, something just on the edge of the portal drew my attention. Squinting, I could see a dark form moving beside the portal, just outside of its boundaries. Was it some kind of ocean creature, curious about the whirling dervish of water?

Except it was moving too fast to be natural.

I kicked my legs to move a little closer to the edge

of the spout. I peered out into the darkness, flinching backwards when the water seemed to gaze back at me. Coldness crept through me, as if something had sliced into my very soul. Someone was out there, moving as quickly as the portal. Curious, I reached out with a hand, the tips of my fingers piercing the veil between ocean and portal.

Then I was sucked out of the vortex. Tossed out like week old garbage.

Panicked, I thrashed around in the cold water, twisting to my left and right, trying to get my bearings. I couldn't see anything around me. The light had vanished. I was alone. My lungs burned. I couldn't hold my breath any longer. I was going to drown in the void of the ocean. No one would ever find my body. Sophia would never know what happened to me. I'd failed before I even got a chance to start.

My chest hurt so badly, I couldn't think beyond it. I had to open my mouth. I had to swallow in the water, let it absorb me. Maybe it wouldn't be too painful to drown; maybe it would all be over in a matter of minutes, if I just succumbed.

A split second before I opened my mouth, I felt strong hands on me. They whipped my body around until I came face to face with the guy who had pulled me out of the water at the pier. He cupped my face with his hands, then leaned in, and pressed his lips to mine. Confused, I didn't know what was happening until I felt the pressure in my head and chest alleviate as he blew oxygen into my body.

Then he grabbed my arm and kicked hard with his legs. A minute later, I was dragged out of the water and up onto a rocky shore. Sputtering and spitting out liquid, I rolled onto my side. Blinking back black spots, I saw we'd come up into a large cave. The rock walls sparkled with some kind of quartz. Thick, sharp looking green-stained stalagmites hung down from the ceiling, dripping water onto the stone floor near me. The plip-plop of the drops echoed off the walls and floor. Beyond them, I could see a large opening where blue and green light beams seemed to dance around.

"Wow, who let her in?"

I blinked away water to see the girl with the long, dark hair snickering at me. Her companion, a plump girl with short blonde hair, shook her head. There was no hiding her disdain. "Her face is as blue as her hair."

I tried to sit up, but my body wasn't behaving. All my limbs felt weighted down. They were too heavy to lift. It was like having swimmer's cramps everywhere at once. This time the guy didn't offer his hand to me, he just yanked me to my feet, none too gently, either.

"Don't look so sad, Blue, you're not dead." He bopped me on the nose with his finger. "Not yet, anyway." He tipped his head then joined the girl with the dark hair and her friend. Together, they walked deeper into the cave toward the opening.

For a split second, I thought about running after him to thank him for saving my life, but I was already mortified about what had happened. I didn't want to give his spite-filled companions an opportunity to run me down even further. So, I just got in line with everyone else as they trudged toward the cave opening. We all looked like drowned rats marching through a sewer.

The guy who had been standing beside me earlier fell in step with me. "Are you okay?"

"Oh yeah, peachy."

"I'm Ren, by the way."

"Melany." I offered him a small smile.

As the opening drew nearer, nerves started zinging through me. This was it. There was no turning back now. A few more steps and I would be completely committing to join the Gods' Army. And the only way out was either by expulsion or death. There was no leaving on one's own accord.

I stepped through the mouth of the cave and into a whole new world. Literally.

The sky was a color of blue I'd never seen before, as bright as a robin's egg. The only clouds in sight hovered in a perfect circle over the massive gray stone building that couldn't be anything other than the academy itself. Sharp spires rose into the sky from round turrets located at all four corners. Large arched windows peppered all three levels of the building. The stain-glassed windows cast beams of green and blue and yellow onto the ground, like lasers.

The wide cobblestone path leading up to the school was lined with spindly trees whose branches should've contained green foliage, but instead were bare. Nothing could possibly grow from the ashen limbs. To the right was a large hedge maze, the entrance guarded by two stone soldiers, their swords raised to fight.

While we walked up the path, Ren audibly swallowed, as he quickly glanced at the statues. "I heard all the stone statues around the academy were once people, turned to stone by the fierce gaze of Medusa. The rumor is if you hear the hiss of snakes, then she's nearby, and you'll be turned to stone next."

I frowned. "I think that's just a stupid story to scare people. Medusa may exist, but she isn't some scary woman walking around with snakes for hair."

"Move it or lose it, recruit."

Someone pushed Ren and me aside, so they could pass by on the path. Two someones. A centaur with long, flowing auburn hair that matched the hair on his horse body, and a tall, thin woman topping six feet, with green tendrils of hair. Hair that seemed to move around her head, as if it was floating in water. I squinted to get a closer look. Were there tiny little faces at the ends of that hair?

She turned to look at me, and her eyes were completely white, devoid of an iris or pupil. She had no eyelashes either, just almond-shaped pale orbs. She smiled, flashing razor-sharp, pointed teeth.

The centaur also glanced back at us, and there was no disguising his distaste in what he saw. "Can you believe the type of misfit they're letting into the academy nowadays? It wasn't like when we trained here."

"That was a few thousand years ago, Chiron. The world has changed."

They both turned back around and kept walking down the path to the academy.

Ren nudged me in the side. "What was that you were saying?"

I gaped, rubbing at my eyes. Was I hallucinating? Had I actually drowned in the ocean, and this was some kind of purgatory? Or were all the rumors and stories about the Gods and the demi-gods who were spawned from them as real as I was?

CHAPTER FOUR

MELANY

*S*till startled by the encounter with Medusa and Chiron, I kept my head down the rest of the way to the academy. I really didn't want to court any more trouble. Deep inside, I thought for sure they somehow knew I didn't belong, being demigods and all, and would out me right there and then before my peers. It hadn't happened, but now I was even more paranoid than before.

The closer we got to the school, the grander and loftier it loomed. From a distance, it had looked maybe three stories tall, but the reality of it when we neared the ornate, ten-foot high wooden doors was like peering up at a great Gothic cathedral or a castle from medieval England, built to withstand any battle siege. It was all dark stone and sharp edges. There was nothing comforting or warm about the place at all.

As the first recruit arrived—naturally it just happened to be the guy who had saved me and his little crew—the huge doors opened, as if on their own, and he and the rest of the recruits walked through, entering the building. When I passed under the high arch of the entrance, a strange vibration rippled over my body, and now I was suddenly dry and so were my clothes and my backpack. I looked around to see if others had felt it, but I couldn't tell, as either they had a look of rapture on their face or abject terror. I didn't think they even noticed they weren't sopping wet anymore.

I decided to stick to Ren's side as we all gathered in the antechamber. I was a mass of nervous energy, unsure of what to do or where to go. But then an excited murmur rippled through the group as a man with long, gray hair and a neatly clipped gray beard leisurely came down the wide stone staircase in front of us.

Beside me, a girl I didn't know grabbed my arm. "It's Zeus," she whispered. "Holy crap."

I craned my neck to get a better view of him as he stood on the steps and looked down at us with an amused quirk of his lips. He didn't look all-powerful or all-knowing. He looked like a tired old man out for a stroll, wearing baggy beige linen pants and a roomy linen tunic. Was he wearing a bathrobe on top?

"Welcome recruits." His voice boomed, echoing all around us. I actually could feel it vibrating against my heart. It was like being next to a huge speaker at a rave, and the DJ was spinning something bass heavy. I rubbed at my sternum, frowning, as he continued to speak.

"You have been invited to the academy because there is something special about you. You have been picked out of millions of young people because somewhere in your family lineage runs Gods' blood."

Oh shit. I'm going to get found out. I most definitely do not have Gods' blood running through my veins.

The girl beside me continued to squeeze my arm, as her excitement grew with his words. "I knew it," she whispered.

"You are stronger, smarter, healthier, more enhanced than the rest of the population, and that is why you are here." His eyes started to glow as his voice rumbled throughout the building. "To train to be the fiercest soldiers to ever set foot on the Earth."

Some of the group clapped, others cheered. I swallowed down the bile rising in my throat, knowing I shouldn't be here. I wondered how easy it would be for me to turn around and walk out of the academy. Would I be stopped?

"Your training will not be easy. It will be the most difficult thing you have ever done. You will be asked to push yourself beyond your limitations. There will be sweat and tears and blood spilled in the halls of this academy before your three years are finished."

I glanced around at all the people surrounding me. Some had glossy, wide eyes, enraptured with Zeus's speech, and others kept their gazes on their feet, maybe too afraid to even look at the God of all Gods. One boy nearby licked his lips nervously. His hands shook at his sides.

My heart pounded so hard I could feel it in my throat, but it wasn't with fear. Exhilaration at the prospect of pushing myself beyond anything I could imagine made my head swim. Maybe here I could prove myself. Prove that I was worth all the cells that combined in complicated patterns to make me a person. Although I was afraid of being found out, I wasn't frightened of sweat, tears, or blood. I'd spilled them already just to get here.

"Your first year will be hard. You will be trained in all disciplines, both physical and mental, so that we may ascertain where your Gods' power and affiliation lies. At the end of the year, you will each have to face twelve harrowing trials. One for each of the Gods. *If* you survive, you will be placed into the corresponding God's clan that you are connected to."

That caused a murmur through the group. I heard various Gods' names spoken out loud. *Poseidon. Athena. Apollo.* I heard one girl near me say, "I'm most definitely in Aphrodite's clan." She was pretty and blonde, and it made me both angry and sad that she thought her look was what was special about her. Everyone was so enthralled with what clan they wanted to belong to they seemed to have missed the, *"If you survive,"* part of that sentence.

I didn't know which of the Gods I aspired to. I

hadn't given it much thought over the years, since I never expected to be called to the academy.

A buzzing filled my ear, like a slight brushing of a finger across the top, or a hushed whisper of words I couldn't quite decipher.

I whipped around to see who had spoken. Someone was messing around. The boy behind me gave me a funny look and then ignored me. I glanced at the girl beside him, but I didn't think she even noticed my presence she was so wrapped up in what Zeus was saying. Had I imagined the voice? It was possible, but it just had been so clear.

"Know this now, not every one of you will succeed here."

That made everyone shut up.

"Some of you will fail. And if you do, you will not just be sent back to your homes. In fact, you will never be able to go back home again. If you fail, you will be expelled from this academy and cursed to live the rest of your life in hardship and misery. No one will take pity on you. No one will help you. You will forever be *the lost*."

Silence consumed the room. I almost covered my mouth, so no one could hear my sharp intake of breath. I heard the ticking of someone's watch and was surprised they even wore one. Every tick got louder and louder until I thought my eardrums would burst.

Then Zeus smiled and clapped his hands together, the sound like thunder, rattling the stones of the foundation of the building. "Now, let's get you settled into your dorms. Also, there's going to be a big party for you in the great hall later, so you can eat, drink, and be merry." His smile grew even wider. "Because come tomorrow, your training will start."

Two other people appeared at the top of the stairs. A man who looked like he just walked off the front page of GQ magazine—short, thick dark hair swept up off his face, chiseled face, cheekbones that could cut glass, a full set of lips made for kissing, and piercing blue eyes framed by dark, square-shaped glasses. He wore a tight turtleneck accentuating all his muscles and simple dark jeans that I imagined hugged a perfect behind. Every girl, even a few guys, swooned at the sight of him. Me included. This had to be Eros.

His female counterpart was equally as attractive—long, dark beach waves, sultry brown eyes, full lips painted red, high cheekbones, regal nose. She wore a simple red dress hugging full breasts and shapely hips. Her long, sculpted legs were perfectly presented in red heels. I suspected she was named Psyche. Every male's gaze was riveted on her.

Smiling, she gestured with her hand to her left. "If the boys would please follow me, I will direct you to your dorm rooms."

There was a mad rush up the stairs. I got jostled by the two boys who had been standing behind me.

"Ladies, if you will come with me." Eros grinned. "I'll show you to your dorms."

Another mad rush up the stairs, this time with a bit of pushing and shoving as girls tried to get to the front of the line and closest to Eros. I was happy to follow along in the back of the pack. Although Eros definitely ticked all my attraction boxes, I wasn't here to fall in love, despite the fact that I couldn't get mystery guy's face out of my head.

As we walked through the long, wide corridors of the living quarters of the academy, Eros chatted casually about the party we would be attending later and how much fun it would be.

"There will be all kinds of amazing food there. And Dionysus is an epic DJ. He helped Daft Punk get their start years ago." He looked left to right suspiciously, then leaned in toward the group. "He used to party with Mozart way back when, but you didn't hear it from me."

One of the girls at the front giggled. "Are you going to be there?"

He gave her a disarming smile. "I might be. Maybe you can save me a dance?"

She giggled again, and I thought for sure she was going to pass out. The girl next to her had to put a hand on her arm to brace her from falling.

"So, here we are, ladies. Your dorm rooms. They aren't assigned, so pick a room as quickly as you can. You don't want to be the odd one out, or you'll have to share a room with Medusa. And she's not very friendly."

Everyone darted to their left or right and into the rooms on either side. There was some shoving near the rooms closest to the stairs, so I hightailed it down the hallway away from everyone else and dashed into a dark room, hoping maybe I'd luck out and not have a roommate. I immediately toppled over whatever it was sitting in the middle of the floor.

"What the fu—"

"Oh, goodness, I'm so sorry."

I sat up, squinting into the darkness. A shadowed form moved about on the floor then stood. Light suddenly flooded the room, and I peered up at a petite girl with short red hair.

I scrambled to my feet. "What were you doing on the floor?"

"Talking to him." She held up a tiny brown mouse by the tail. "I was telling him he needed to find another place to live."

That was when I noticed the state of the room. Cobwebs covered each corner, both ceiling and floor. Dust coated everything else, including the small desk by the grimy window and the two beds that were stacked up on one another along one wall. And I didn't even want to identify the tiny pebbles on the floor. Considering this girl was holding up a tiny rodent, I didn't have to try too hard to figure it out.

She must've seen the disgust on my face. "It'll be nice once we clean it up and fix the beds." She held out her other hand to me. "I'm Georgina Thrace, by the way."

"Melany Richmond." After we shook hands, I took off my backpack and set it down on the floor, glancing around. "I wonder where we'll find a broom."

She smiled.

An hour later, we'd cleaned the room and made our respective beds. Georgina proved to be incredibly strong and pretty much did all the heavy lifting when it came to organizing where our beds were going to go. I was surprised, considering she looked more chubby than sturdy.

Once we were done, I felt my stomach growl. I didn't even know what time it was, as my phone didn't seem to be working any longer. I didn't know if it was because it got water damaged or if it was this place. We sure weren't in Kansas anymore.

"I'm starving. Do you want to go down to this party and get some food?"

Georgina nodded. "I could most definitely eat."

We left our room and followed some of the other girls who looked like they were making their way to the great hall, wherever that was. Eros left out that detail when he was giving us the quick tour. But as soon as we went down the large stone staircase, we heard the thumping strains of dance music.

We wound our way through empty rooms and hallways toward the sound. The moment we turned the corner of one hallway, there was no mistaking where the party was. The end of the corridor opened up into a cavernous hall made from dark gray stone with a domed ceiling, held up by stone pillars with decorative inlays.

The hall was packed with people. Both new recruits and other students I assumed were second and third year, milled about, talking and laughing. I marveled at it all. I'd never experienced anything like it. Every big party Callie ever had at her house paled in comparison.

My stomach growled again, reminding me of my initial goal. To eat. I looked around for any tables that had food on them but didn't see any immediately. What I did see were small wooden robots rolling around the room on wheels. They each carried a tray with some kind of food on it. I made a bee-line straight for one that had tiny sandwiches.

In my haste, I nearly knocked it over, as I grabbed four sandwiches and shoved them into my mouth. I looked down at the wooden server. Its beady-eyed gaze was on me; I swore there was judgment in that look, which was impossible as it wasn't even alive. I made a grab for one more sandwich before it rolled away from me.

I walked through the party, taking in the people bouncing to the music. It wasn't what I normally liked; I usually went for something a bit more thrashy, a whole lot more metal, but it was decent. My social skills were non-existent, so I kept to the outskirts of the festivity, preferring to watch than do. But my gaze honed in on a pretty black girl being ruthlessly and relentlessly hit on in one of the corners of the room.

Her body language screamed, "Go away!" but the guy wasn't listening. And he was big, too. Muscular, tall, he loomed over her, leering like a creep, trying to touch her long, dark curls. I didn't like the situation one bit. I moved closer to gauge what was going on.

"Please, leave me alone. I told you I don't want to dance." She tried to step around him, but he got in her way.

"We could go out into the courtyard and make out then, if you don't want to dance."

She tried to push past him again, but this time he grabbed her arm. Hell no. Not on my watch.

"She told you to leave her alone." I moved in to stand beside the girl. "You either don't understand English or you're stupid."

"Mind your own business." As he scowled down at me, I realized just how big he was.

"Okay, so you speak English fine, so I guess you're just stupid then."

I saw his attack in my mind before he even moved.

He lunged forward, swinging his right arm at me. I leaned back out of his reach, grabbed his wrist with both hands, tugged him forward, and then swept his back leg with my right one. He was down on the floor in seconds. There were a few people around us, and they started to laugh, as the guy sputtered in surprise on the ground.

I took the girl's hand and pulled her away. We joined a bunch of people on the dance floor.

Smiling, she bent towards my ear. "Oh my Gods, thank you for coming to my rescue."

"Any time. I can't stand bullies."

"I'm Jasmine."

"Melany."

"Isn't this all nuts?" She gestured to the chaos

happening all around us, and I imagined she was talking about the whole situation we'd stepped into.

The DJ, who had spiked up black hair and wore black eyeliner, jumped up onto one of the serving robots and rode it around in front of his set up, flailing his arms around. "Who's ready to get crazy?"

Everyone on the dance floor screamed in response. Then he did a backflip off the robot, ran back to his turntable, and dropped another thumping song sending everyone into a frenzy. I couldn't help but be swept up as well. The music was infectious, getting right into my muscles and bones.

I danced with Jasmine, moving my body to each oscillating pulse of music. I jumped up and down, turned, and nearly collided with my savior from earlier. He grinned at me, which made my belly flip flop.

"Having a good time, Blue?"

"Yes. Are you?"

"I'll let you know in a minute." He reached for my hand and was about to pull me close, when the dark-haired girl interrupted, getting right in between us. He dropped my hand.

"You're not slumming it, are you, Lucian?" She gave me a side-eye, clearly disgusted with everything about me. In lots of ways, she reminded me of Callie.

Anger swelled inside me, and I needed to get away before I did something I'd regret. I didn't need to get expelled from the academy before classes even started. I walked off the dance floor and searched for a place to sit away from the celebration. But everyone was in full party mode. The music, the smell of the food and drink, and the heat of so many people crushed together pushed down on me. I needed some air.

I left the great hall with the intention of finding a way outside, but the sound of footsteps approaching had me pressing up against a shadowed wall. I didn't want to get into trouble for leaving the celebration. I had a sense this place was big on rules with harsh punishments.

I peeked around the corner to see literally a blonde Goddess walking down the empty corridor. She was tall, six feet at least, yards of golden waves trailing down her back to her tiny waist. The hem of her sheer white dress dragged behind her like the train of a wedding gown or a royal gown. She definitely was regal.

After she moved down the hallway a little farther away, she stopped and turned. Even from where I hid, I could see how stunning she was. Her face looked like it was sculpted from the whitest, hardest marble to ever exist, and her eyes were as blue as the hottest part of a flame. This had to be Aphrodite. The stories about her beauty didn't even come close to the reality of her.

I wasn't sure what she was doing, but I didn't have to wait long until another form stepped out from a different darkened corridor. It was a man, a mountainous muscular man with a shaved head. He looked like an army drill sergeant on steroids. They embraced, kissing. Obviously, there was something going on there.

But the way she kept looking around, it was definitely a secret something.

"Were you followed?" Aphrodite asked her lover.

He shook his head. "Does Hephaistos suspect anything?"

"He wouldn't notice if I came home dipped in blood. All he cares about is his toys and contraptions."

"Then he'd never noticed the key was gone?"

I leaned around the corner, eager to get closer.

"Not for the time we'd need to open…" Pausing, she whipped her head around to where I hid.

I jerked backward, the heel of my boot squeaking against the polished tile floor. *Shit.*

I didn't wait to see if they heard me. I hightailed it out of there. The very last thing I needed was a couple of Gods thinking I'd overheard their clandestine meeting to discuss evil doings.

CHAPTER FIVE

MELANY

*T*he loudest, most resonant gong ever to exist literally knocked me out of bed in the morning.

From the spot I landed on the cold, hard floor, I could see through the dorm room window that it was still dark out. I swore I hadn't even been asleep for more than four hours.

"Time to rise and shine." Georgina's face loomed over me. In the predawn, I noticed she was already dressed in the official academy uniform, dark red polo and charcoal gray military style pants with side pockets. She looked sufficiently groomed and ready to attack the day.

I, on the other hand, still had sleep gluing my eyelashes together.

She offered her hand to me to help me up and I took it. "Do you always look this bright-eyed in the morning?"

"Yes, pretty much. I love early mornings. I like to be productive."

I sat on the edge of my bed and rubbed at the crusty flakes in my eyes. "Back home, I wouldn't even be out of bed until noon."

"If I were you, I'd get your butt in gear and run to the showers before they fill up. Or you won't be able to have one before we need to be in our first class." She handed me a thick leather folder. "Here's your class schedule. I hope you don't mind that I organized it for you. I had an hour to kill this morning before the gong."

I opened it to see a calendar and detailed timetable noting my classes and which professors taught them. As I perused my schedule for the day, I shook my head. I couldn't believe this was happening. I couldn't believe I was here, at the academy, training to be in the Gods' Army.

8 a.m.
– History of the Gods – Hera
10 a.m. – Spear and Shield – Ares
12 p.m. – lunch
1 p.m. – Archery - Artemis
3 p.m. – Hand to Hand Combat – Heracles
5 p.m. – dinner

7 p.m. – Prophecy – Apollo
9 p.m. – free time
11 p.m. – lights out

I kept reading, marveling at the other classes during the week.

"Transformation class?" I looked up at Georgina, dumbfounded. "What the hell do we do in that class?"

"I guess we make one thing into another."

I looked back at the schedule. "Flying?" I shook my head. "Tomorrow, we have an elemental class with Zeus and Poseidon."

"I know, right? I'm so excited for that one. Demeter teaches in that class, too. I've wanted to meet her my entire life. My family has made offerings to her since I was a baby."

I wanted to tell her that most likely the Goddess never got them, but what did I know? For most of my life, I didn't even think the Gods were real. I'd been told they were real. I read about them in picture books for children, been instructed on how to worship them, and what to take to what temple to pray. But I never truly, honestly believed there were higher beings sitting around listening to the whining and bitching of mortals. And here I was in their school, training to fight for them in some war that didn't exist. At least none that I knew about.

A half hour later, I, along with Georgina and twenty other girls, streamed down the main stone staircase and into the foyer where we first had entered the academy. The boys came from the opposite way, where their dorms were, and joined us on the stairs. I saw Jasmine near the front of the group. Hopefully, I'd be able to catch up with her.

At the bottom of the steps, we were met by an assuming woman with curly brown hair up in a messy bun, a very plain dress, and sensible shoes. She looked like a librarian. She even had reading glasses hanging on a chain around her neck.

She smiled warmly at us. "Good morning. My name is Pandora, and I'll be your guide for the day. I will show you to your various classes and answer any questions you may have about the academy. I'm your TA for the year. If you need anything, you can come to me."

She led us down a very large, wide corridor—the whole academy seemed to consist of enormous corridors—to a set of gray stone doors with stars engraved into them.

"This is where your history of the Gods class will be. It's a very important class, as you will need to know everything you can about each of the primary Gods and Goddesses to prepare for your trial at the end of the year."

A tall girl with blond hair raised her hand.

Pandora smiled at her. "Yes?"

"Are the trials as bad as they say? I heard that a boy died during the trial of Zeus."

Others in the group looked around nervously.

Pandora gave us a tight-lipped smile. "Rumors don't do anyone any good." She gestured to the doors. "Have a good class, and I'll see you afterwards."

The doors swung open, and we all entered the dark room. I wondered if anyone else noticed Pandora didn't exactly answer the question. Probably not, as everyone was busy gawking at the domed ceiling above us. It was lit up with a thousand twinkling stars.

In the center of the room stood a rising platform, and around it were fifty desks and chairs. There was a scramble for the desks in the middle, but I opted for one farthest from the lectern. Georgina followed me to the back. As I slid behind my desk, I was pleasantly surprised to see Jasmine taking a desk in front of me. We smiled at each other.

Another door at the far end of the room opened and a woman entered. I assumed it was Hera, our professor. She walked to the center of the room and stepped up onto the dais. She wore a long, flowing dark blue dress, and her hair was wrapped up on top of her head with a string of flowers acting like a turban. Jewels sparkled around her throat, her ears, and her fingers, as she lifted her hands in front of her.

"Everything in the cosmos was created by Uranus and Gaia, Heaven and Earth." Between her hands, light formed. She twisted her hands around until a solid ball of blue erupted then she threw it up at the ceiling. The orb bounced from one star to the next and the next, sending them all spinning, until they were a spiraling mass of stars and light above us.

There were gasps around the room as the stars separated and rotated into position in the universe. Then one star grew ten times its initial size into a large globe. Land and sea formed on as it turned on its axis. It was the Earth.

"Heaven and Earth gave birth to twelve great, ferocious and ruthless Titans. Oceanus…"

The thundering sounds of crashing waves filled the room. Then a swirling blue maelstrom spouted from the floor. Some of the students nearest to it jumped out of their seats and screamed. It looked so real; I expected to be sprayed by water as it spun through the room, turning into a gigantic monster made of water, with eight whirlpool arms spinning around.

"…dominated all the seas and oceans and lakes and rivers, demolishing ships and drowning everyone he came in contact with.

"Hyperion, made of the sun itself…"

Out from the ceiling dropped a male form made of fire, with huge fiery wings. A wave of heat surged through the room with every flap of his wings. He lifted his arms, which were columns of fire, and shot out fireballs every direction. One fireball zoomed straight for my head and I ducked. I could actually feel the heat as it flew by, vanishing when it hit the stone wall.

"…scorched everything in his path…"

For the next hour, Hera introduced all twelve Titans and talked about how monstrous and destructive they were. Then she talked about Tartarus, the stinking, dark, frozen wasteland they were imprisoned in, a place far below the underworld, and how important it was for the Gods to make sure they stayed there.

"This is why you are being trained," she said, her voice rising to a crescendo. "You will be the Gods' Army, to fight by our side in the event our enemies are unleashed on the Earth."

A chill ran through me, as I thought about the repercussions of any of the Titans being released from their prison, and why someone would ever want that to happen. It made me think about what I had overheard in the academy halls last night.

After history class, Jasmine and I met up.

"That class was crazy, huh?"

I nodded. "Yeah, seems so unreal."

Georgina came along my other side. "It's as real as you and me."

I introduced her to Jasmine, and the three of us followed Pandora and the rest of the group to our next class—Spear and Shield—which was outside behind the main academy building in an open grass field. As we lined up in a semi-circle, three men ran out onto the field, shouting and making shiver-inducing battle cries. All three carried a long spear with an arrowhead-like tip and a round shield. I assumed one of them had to be our professor, Ares.

Two of the men, dressed in black military fatigues, attacked the third man, who was older, and wearing red nylon shorts and a white tank top. His hair was cut short, much like an army general. I remembered him from the hallway last night. This had to be Ares.

As I watched him dance around the field, deflecting blows from the other men, he reminded me of my old gym teacher from high school who loved to play dodgeball. I swore it was his most favorite activity. He'd probably even slept with the dodgeball clutched tight in his hands, like a child with his little stuffed toy.

The image made me snicker. I put a hand up to my mouth to stifle it, but it was too late. It had already escaped, and a couple of the people around me noticed, and basically took a step away from me, singling me out.

After Ares made a sharp cutting motion with his hand, the other two men immediately stopped what they were doing and stood at attention with their shield held at chest height, and their spear held upright in their hand, eyes forward, chins lifted. Ares spun around and glared at me.

Obviously, he had also noticed my snicker.

He pointed right at me. "Step forward."

I gestured to myself. "Me?"

"Yes. Get out here. Now!"

I stepped out of the group and onto the field. Both Georgina and Jasmine looked horrified, while the dark-haired girl, whose name I discovered during history class was Revana, openly smirked.

Ares tossed his shield at me. I put my arm up just in time to catch it before it smashed me in the head. It was heavy, and I had a hard time keeping it balanced. Then he thrust his spear at me.

"Protect yourself!"

I raised the shield just in time, so the spear tip didn't pierce my face. It bounced off the metal. "What the hell?"

He thrust it toward me again, this time at my legs. I managed to move the big metal plate down in time, and the clang of metal hitting metal reverberated over my entire body. My arm shook, and I nearly dropped the shield.

"Do you find this funny?" he shouted at me.

"No!"

He lowered his spear and took a step back to address the entire group. "War is not funny." He tapped the spear onto the ground. "There will be no laughing in my class. Do you understand?"

"Yes," some of the group said.

"Do you understand?"

"Yes sir!"

He came back to me and tore the shield from my hand. "Get back in line."

Head down, I quickly walked back to the group, standing next to Georgina and Jasmine. Jasmine leaned in. "Are you okay?"

I rotated my right shoulder; it was starting to ache from holding the shield up. I nodded. "I'll live."

"Form two lines." Ares gestured with his hand where we should line up. "You are going to learn how to use a shield properly to defend yourself, so you don't get stuck in the gut with a spear and bleed out."

We all jumped into motion. I wanted to get in line with Georgina and Jasmine, but ended up getting jostled around, until I could squeeze into a line, which just happened to be beside Lucian. Perfect. This day was just getting worse and worse by the minute. I could just imagine the joke he was going to make at my expense.

He bent toward me. "Not bad, Blue."

I didn't look at him, keeping my eyes ahead. "Oh yeah, I was a real hero there. I'll be defending the masses in no time."

"Hey, I know it's not easy holding one of those shields up."

When I turned to look at him, I noticed the long, thin scar along his jawline.

He rubbed his thumb across it, then he winked at me, and I couldn't stop the smile blossoming on my face.

Then a shadow loomed over me.

"I said no laughing during class." Ares glared at me, his scowl so deep it cut lines into his granite-like face.

"Technically, I wasn't laughing. I was smiling."

He got right into my face. I had to crane my neck to look up at him. He was so close I could smell his body odor.

"You need to check your attitude, Blue Belle, or I'm going to rip that nose ring right out of your face."

The intensity of his anger rippled over me. I didn't like how it felt on my skin. Like snakes, a thousand tiny snakes slithering over my body, every muscle quiver constricting me tighter and tighter.

"To help you with this lesson, I want you to go out in the middle of the field and do some pushups. You will keep doing them until I tell you to stop. Do you hear what I'm saying to you, recruit?"

"Yes, sir."

Revana, who was nearby, started to snicker.

"Sounds like someone else is laughing, sir."

Ares whipped around and glared at Revana. "You can join her."

I walked out onto the field and dropped down to my hands and knees. Revana followed me out and nearly stepped on my hand as she took up a position beside me. As we both did our first pushup, she glowered at me, her eyes like dark storm clouds.

"I know you're a fraud. When I find out how you got in here, I'm going straight to Zeus, and you'll be expelled from the academy and exiled from your life."

"Wow, girl, you really need to relax. You are much too tense."

As she did pushups, she continued to glare at me. I didn't know how one person could put so much effort into hating someone they didn't even know. It must be exhausting.

It was just another reason, in a long list of them, of why coming here was a bad idea, and one I was sure I was going to regret. I should've given the box back to Callie, and maybe she'd be the one on the ground doing pushups until she puked.

CHAPTER SIX

LUCIAN

*D*espite all my past training, the reality of the academy and what we were being put through paled in comparison. Walking into the gymnasium for hand-to-hand combat class and seeing Heracles, the giant of a man who stood seven feet tall and was built like a semi-truck, training us crushed any confidence I had going in. This was in no way going to be an easy class.

All my life, I'd been training for the possibility of being invited to join the Gods' Army. For my parents, it was inevitable since my older brother, Owen, had been called four years earlier by his eighteenth birthday Shadowbox. I hadn't seen or heard from him since the day he'd left, as recruits were cut off from the outside world. In the back of my mind, I had hoped he'd be here at the academy when I arrived. But that hope had been dashed when I realized that those who had completed the training and gone through the trials transcended to Olympus to await the Great War. Maybe I would see him again when I, too, transcended.

Since I was six years old, my father had started training me in various disciplines like archery, deep sea diving, and hand-to-hand combat. And my parents had placed offerings at the temple of Ares since I'd been born in the hopes I would become part of his clan. Like my brother had. Or at least, I assumed he had.

"Form a single line," Heracles bellowed, his voice echoing off the dark wooden floors and paneled walls.

Everyone rushed to get side by side. My friend, Diego, made sure to get next to me. Revana pushed another girl aside, so she could get in on my other side. The girl could be ruthless, which I didn't like, but I supposed a person had to be to get through this training.

I looked down the line and spotted Melany about ten people away. I wasn't sure what to make of her. She seemed so much out of her element, like she didn't truly belong. From misreading where the entrance to the academy was, to diving out of the portal and nearly drowning, to talking back to Ares. I'd never thought anyone with any kind of smarts would ever risk that. She intrigued me; that was for certain.

"The first thing we are going to learn in this class is stance, how to keep your center of gravity. If you perfect this, you will never be knocked off balance, no matter how you move or what hits you." He moved to the center of the floor and put his left leg forward, toe pointing straight, and his back foot pointing outwards. He bent his legs a little and then put up his hands to his chest, hugging his arms a little into his sides.

"Now, from here, I can perform any kind of maneuver." He did a jab, and then upper cut, then threw an elbow, then he spun on his foot and did a back kick, coming back to rest in the same position. He moved so quickly, his limbs blurred.

Beside me, Diego sucked in a breath. "Damn. I've never seen anyone move so fast."

"In this stance, nothing can knock me over."

From the far back corners of the room, two six-foot tall wooden dummy robots on wheels rolled toward Heracles. Both carried long wooden Bo staffs. One of the robots rolled in front of Heracles, lifted its arms, the staff reared back as far as it would go, then it swung with all its power.

Heracles lifted his arm, tight to his body; the staff smacked him across the shoulder, the cracking sound reverberating off every surface, and snapped in half. Splinters of wood rained down onto the floor.

He grinned, his whole demeanor changing, as the second staff hit him in the other side, and snapped into pieces from the force of the blow. He straightened and brushed off the small wood chips still clinging onto his shirt. "Ha!" He pumped his fist in the air. "I am invincible. Nothing can knock me off balance. Now, it's your turn."

I heard a snicker down the line. I didn't need to look to know it was Melany.

"You're seriously going to smack us with wooden staffs?" She had her hands on her hips and appeared indignant. Her lips were curled in disgust.

Heracles shook his head. "Of course not. It's only the first day. I don't do that until at least week four."

That got a round of laughs through the group.

"Take up your stances."

I put my left leg forward, and my back leg turned like I'd practiced over and over again since I was six. The others around me all did the same, as Heracles walked down the line and inspected us. He spoke to a couple of people, correcting them, and then when he got to me, he stopped. He looked me over and then shoved me hard.

I stumbled a couple of steps backward, but I didn't break my stance. I didn't lose my balance.

He nodded. "Good. Step forward."

I did.

"Name?"

"Lucian Remes."

Heracles's eyes narrowed. "You have a brother."

"Yes, Owen." My heart leapt a little, knowing that Owen had made some kind of impression. He would've done well in this class.

"I want you to go down the line and try to knock down every person." Heracles glanced at the rest of the group. "Your job is to not let him." He pointed to the far end of the room where a short blonde girl stood.

I walked down the line and stood in front of her. Fear clouded her eyes, and I felt bad for doing what I had to. It didn't take much to knock her onto her ass.

One by one, I pushed and shoved my fellow recruits. Some stayed on their feet, most fell. When I got to Diego, I had a feeling he thought I'd go easy on him. I didn't. He lost his balance after one hard shove. Revana kept her feet, even after two hard pushes from different angles. She grinned at me in triumph.

When I reached Melany, she looked like she was already ready to go to war. The fierce expression in her eyes made my gut clench. But I didn't think it had anything to do with being afraid of her.

"You ready?"

"Take your best shot." She lifted her chin in defiance.

I came at her from the side and pushed on her shoulder. She stayed pretty much in place. I tried again from the front. As I stretched my arms toward her, she stepped into me and swept my leg. I ended up on my ass. A ripple of laughter went through the room.

Stunned, I gaped up at her. She shrugged and offered her hand to help me up. "He said to not let you knock me down. So I didn't."

I grabbed her hand, and she pulled me to my feet. I felt a buzz of something not entirely unpleasant on the palm of my hand. I quickly let her hand go and rubbed it on my pants. The skin still tingled.

"Oh, I like this one." Clapping, Heracles walked over. "Name?"

"Melany Richmond."

"Melany, the dark one. I love it." He looked at the rest of the group. "All right, everyone pair up. We're going to learn to spar." He pointed at me and Melany. "Congratulations, you two are now partners."

When he moved away, we gaped at each other.

"We are going to learn how to jab, cross, and uppercut properly. Three fundamental punches in your arsenal. One of you grab a pair of focus pads from the wall, then we will start."

I looked at Melany. She sighed. "I'll go get them." Then she jogged to the far wall and grabbed a couple of rectangular pads and came back.

I took them from her. "You can practice first." I slid my hands into the holders and lifted them up in front of my body.

"Get in your stances," Heracles instructed. "Then we will practice a jab, cross, jab." He demonstrated, smacking huge fists into pads that one of the wooden dummy robots held up. I was surprised he didn't break the robot with his punches.

Melany got into position, then jabbed my one pad, then did a cross punch with her left, then another jab. Her punches were solid, and I liked that she didn't seem to hold back.

I nodded. "Not bad, Blue."

"Thanks."

She did it again and again, landing every punch with power. I could feel the zing of her fists even through the pads. It was impressive.

"Switch!" Heracles shouted.

I took off the pads and handed them to her. She slid them on and raised them up. I got into my stance and led with a jab. I may have not put all my weight behind it, and I think she must've known because she gave me a disgusted look.

"I'm not fragile. You're not going to break me into little pieces."

"Are you sure? You are kind of small."

She shook her head. "You really do have a big ego, don't you?"

I shrugged. "No bigger than most."

Her lips twitched, but she fought back the smile.

I took up my stance again and jabbed with full power. Her arm snapped back a little, but then she pushed it forward, so I could hit the pad again. I did. Then I was doing my sequence of punches without any hesitation.

By the time Heracles yelled to stop, sweat covered my face and rolled down my back. It was the same for Melany.

"Woe ho ho, looks like we got ourselves a dream team here." Heracles grinned at both of us. "Keep up the good work." He smacked me on the shoulder, and I stumbled backward, but not before I caught Melany snickering.

"Are you laughing at me?" I gave her a searching look.

"No, of course not." Sarcasm dripped off her like the sweat dripped off her brow.

At first I'd been hesitant to be paired up with her. I thought she would slow me down somehow. But the truth was we made kind of an awesome team. It was both surprising and unnerving. There was something about Melany that unsettled me. It was more than just her unconventional good looks, her dark blue hair begging me to touch it; it went deeper than that. She was different in many ways. In ways I think she didn't even realize.

I'd spent my entire life around true believers. I'd been training for the day I got invited to the army. There had never been a question whether I would or not. I was certain that I had Gods' blood in my veins. I suspected that my friends had Gods' blood as well.

And here was this girl, who looked completely and utterly out of place, and I wasn't sure she even truly believed she should be here, but out of every first year recruit, I was sure she had more reason to be at the academy than anyone.

CHAPTER SEVEN

MELANY

There was a buzz of excitement and nervousness as we descended a large stone staircase into the deepest and darkest part of the academy. Everyone was psyched to go to metallurgy class with Hephaistos. Everyone except me. I just wanted to go back to my dorm room and hide under the covers. I'd had a day of embarrassing blunders and didn't really want to suffer through any more.

The morning's archery class with Artemis had been mortifying. I'd wanted to impress Artemis, as she was badass. During the demonstration, the way she moved, so gracefully, so flawlessly, as she sprinted across the training field and shot three arrows into a moving target, rendered me speechless. I wanted to do that. I wanted to be that skilled.

But as it turned out, I had no skill whatsoever for the bow. During training, I couldn't even hit the static target. All my arrows had limply hit the ground in front of them. The first few I understood. I mean, not everyone had hit the target on the first few tries. But even after an hour of pulling back the bow, I still couldn't hit anything but grass, while almost the entire class had at least struck the target. Jasmine had gotten a bullseye and Artemis's praise.

The disparaging looks and cruel snickers I'd gotten from Revana and her crew had nearly reduced me to tears from frustration. I didn't cry, though. I refused to, especially in front of them.

Jasmine nudged me in the side as we walked down the stairs. She knew how upset I was. "You'll get it next time. No one is expecting you to be great the first week of training."

"You were."

"I guess it's just my thing." She shrugged. "Anyway, you more than kicked ass during hand-to-hand combat. And you made Heracles pump his fist and clap. From what I heard, he's not an easy person to impress."

"I had help," I wanted to say, as I spotted Lucian on the stairs in front of me. He was with his usual group, Diego, Revana, and a couple others I didn't know. Why did he hang around them? They were all kind of mean, and he wasn't. At least he wasn't with me. They were laughing about something, probably making fun of someone, then his head turned, and his gaze met mine

and my belly clenched. I immediately turned away, but the sensation still lingered.

I peered down the long, winding staircase. It felt like we'd been walking on them for an hour already. "How many floors down are we going?"

"I heard the forge is deep in the bowels of the earth." This from Georgina, who'd been quiet until now.

Jasmine and I snickered.

"Bowels of the earth?" I gave my roommate a look. "Seriously?"

She shrugged.

Mia, who was in the room one down from Georgina and I, came along Jasmine's other side. "You were so good in archery, Jasmine."

"Thank you." She dipped her head a little, as if she was embarrassed.

As Mia moved on down a couple of stairs from us, Jasmine watched her.

I nudged Jasmine. "So, what's going on there?"

"Nothing." She frowned.

"Looked like something."

"Oh, like the something you have with Lucian?"

I was about to sputter a protest when we finally reached the bottom of the stairs. I turned to look back from where we came. We were at least five or six stories below the main academy.

Pandora led us down a long corridor. It looked more like a tunnel carved into a mountain, as the sides and ceiling weren't smooth, but rough with pieces of rock jutting out. With each step forward, the air around me seemed to be getting warmer. I noticed beads of sweat on Georgina's forehead. Bright orange light flickered ahead in the distance. The sounds of machinery thundered all around as we neared Hephaistos's classroom.

There was a wave of gasps as the tunnel opened up, and we stepped into a cavernous space. I couldn't even call it a room, as it was way too expansive. Stone steps led to bridges hovering over rivers of what I assumed was molten metal, linking various large, circular platforms. Past the biggest platform, bellows puffed, fanning the flames in a forge; its opening mimicked that of a mouth of a black dragon.

Above on the nearest platform, a man stepped out from the steam and smoke of the churning foundry. "Welcome to the forge." His voice was as baritone and resonant as the huge gears turning nearby.

Beside me, Jasmine grabbed my hand. "I don't want to be here."

"It'll be fine. What's the worst that can happen?"

"Technically, you could fall off one of the bridges and into the fire."

I frowned at Georgina, letting her know she wasn't helping.

Carefully, as a group, as everyone seemed to be a bit on edge, we went up the stone stairs and over a bridge to the platform nearest the dragon furnace. I kept my eyes straight ahead; I didn't want to tempt fate by looking over the edge of the bridge. There were several long rectangular stone crafting tables and bowls of fire at the ends. On top of the tables were various sized hammers, iron tongs, and metal files. Near the bowls of fire were several anvils.

We lined up behind the tables, as our professor took up a spot in front of the dragon. On close inspection, I could see that Hephaistos wasn't a pleasant looking person. He appeared a bit misshapen, especially his face and head. Longish, curly brown hair couldn't hide the scar running along his scalp. And his thick mustache couldn't cover the cleft in his lip.

"In this class," he bellowed above the rumble of the foundry behind him, "you will be forging your own personal shield. This shield you will use in various classes and one day out on the battlefield. By third year, the crest of your assigned clan will be proudly embellished on the metal."

"Cool," one of the guys at the table said.

Hephaistos glared in his direction. "The first thing you will learn in this class is that I don't tolerate jokers. There will be no tomfoolery or shenanigans."

Diego, who was at the other table, chuckled.

Hephaistos picked up the closest thing to him, which looked like a blade for a spear, and launched it at Diego. "What did I just say?"

Diego ducked in time, and the spearhead stuck into the stone pillar behind him with a loud thwack.

"To get started, everyone look under the table top, and you will find a cubby hole. Inside, you will find a pair of leather gloves. Put them on or else you will burn your fingers off. And what use will you be without any fingers?"

Over the next hour, Hephaistos showed us how to heat up and bend metal, using the forge and an anvil. Then as a group from each table we got to approach the main forge, stick a hunk of metal into the fire with iron tongs, and then take it over to one of the anvils and hammer it until it bent in half. In theory, it looked and sounded pretty easy. But I couldn't seem to get it right. Like with archery, I didn't possess the right skills. Soon, someone was going to point this out and kick me out of the academy.

I hammered at the glowing part of the metal piece I had, but it didn't bend the way I wanted it to.

"What are you doing?" Hephaistos loomed over me.

"I'm doing what you showed us."

"Then you must be blind, stupid girl. You are doing it all wrong." He snatched the hammer from me, and the tongs holding my metal, and struck at it on the anvil. With three sharp blows, the metal bent in half. Glowering at me, he handed the hammer and tongs back. "Do it again."

I carried my piece of metal back to the fire. Holding it over the heat, I watched as it melted, creating the tell-tale orange glow. Before I moved back to the anvil, something beyond the foundry caught my eye. There were several shelves along one of the only walls in the room, stacked with various metallic objects. Objects I assumed Hephaistos had made—swords, daggers, a flail, a mace even... and Shadowboxes. There was one long shelf with them, each of them different in size and design.

"For Hades's sake girl, it's going to drip into the fire!"

I turned abruptly and nearly dropped the metal piece. As I passed by the other table of recruits, Revana smirked at me and mouthed, "Loser."

It took all I had not to go over there and shove these tongs right up her—

"Girl, get a move on."

I hustled back to the anvil and hammered at my metal piece. This time I got the hang of it, and it bent the way it should have. I looked up at Hephaistos for approval.

His brow furrowed. "I'm not your mother. I'm not going to tell you what a good job you've done."

Anger swelled inside me. I was tired of getting pushed around today. "My mother's dead."

Hephaistos's eyebrows went up, but he didn't say anything, and just moved on to another anvil, to berate another recruit.

When class was over, I shuffled along with the rest of the group out of the forge and back up the seem-ingly non-ending spiraling staircase. At the top, everyone scattered in different directions, as it was our free time slot.

"We're going to the dining hall," Jasmine said. "I heard pizza is on the menu tonight."

"I'll catch up with you. I need to get something from my room."

Jasmine's eyes narrowed at me. I thought for a moment she was going to tell me she'd go with me. "Okay, see you in a bit." She left with Georgina and a couple of other girls.

When they were gone, and the front hall had cleared completely, I crept back down the stairs. I wanted to get a closer look at those Shadowboxes. I wanted to know how they were made. I needed to know their secrets.

When I reached the entrance to the foundry, I stopped and peered into the gloom, making sure Hephaistos was gone or at least in a place where he wouldn't see me. I waited for five minutes, and when I didn't see or hear him, I mounted the stone steps and rushed across the bridge.

In my haste, I didn't see the loose stone, and I tripped over it. My heart leapt into my throat as I nearly keeled over the bridge. At the last second, I pushed off with my legs and jumped, arms pinwheeling, praying to every God and Goddess I could recall in a few seconds that I didn't land in the molten metal.

I fell onto my knees on the next platform. Closing my eyes and counting my blessings, I took a few seconds to catch my breath. I opened my eyes and glanced over at the bridge. It had to have been no less than fifteen feet away. How the heck had I just jumped more than fifteen feet? I shook my head to clear it and then ran over to the shelves before I got caught.

My fingers ached to touch the Shadowboxes. They were so beautiful, so exquisite. I reached for one when I felt a presence behind me. I whipped around and came face to face with Hephaistos.

"What are you doing here?"

"I… I had to look at the boxes. They're so beautiful."

His face softened at little. "You're probably wondering how someone so grotesque made something so magnificent."

"No, I…"

"I think about that all the time." He picked up one of the boxes. "It is my curse, I suppose."

"Did you make all the Shadowboxes?"

He nodded. "Yes, every last one of them. I would've made the one that came to you."

"How do they work?"

He eyed me for a moment and then opened the box for me to see inside. "After you open the box, a scroll appears. On the scroll will be an invitation and etched inside the box a riddle for you to solve, so you can find the location of the portal to the academy." He snapped the box closed. "But of course, you know all that, since you're here."

I couldn't give myself away, but I had to know the truth. "Is there a way to trick the box? To come to the academy on someone else's invitation?"

He snorted. "Absolutely not. That would be impossible. The box will only respond to its intended recipient. One of the Gods couldn't even break the magic tied to the box."

I gnawed at my lip. The relief was so instant that tears welled in my eyes.

"Besides that, the portal only opens for those who are supposed to come to the academy. A person could swim to Atlantis and never find it."

I nodded to him, trying hard not to sob with elation at the fact that I was supposed to be here. That I was invited by the Gods to train in the Gods' Army. That they wanted me, Melany Richmond, poor orphan girl, rebel, trouble-maker, and not Callie Demos, the perfect specimen of Greek devotion, to come to the legendary academy.

He set the box back onto the shelf.

"Thank you, Hephaistos, sir."

I couldn't stop the smile spreading on my face. I turned to head back to the stairs.

"I saw your leap earlier."

I froze, unsure of what to say.

"That was sixteen feet, give or take a few inches." He rubbed at his bulbous nose.

I stared at him, wondering if somehow I had broken even more rules or had broken something when I jumped.

"It was impressive." He gave me a dismissive wave of his meaty hand. "Now, get the hell out of my foundry, and if you ever come here unsupervised again, I'll have you expelled."

I almost ran out of there but was careful on the

bridge this time. As I mounted the stairs, my heart was hammering as loud as the one I'd used earlier. I vibrated with excitement. I wasn't the outcast I thought I was. I had every right to be here. The knowledge of that propelled me up the stairs two at a time.

When I reached the top, I had a skip in my step and was going to go to the dining hall and eat as much pizza as I could fit into my mouth. As I came around the corner, a hand clamped over my mouth, and I was pushed up against the wall. Instinct took over and I lashed out, biting down on the hand over my lips.

"Ow, Blue. You didn't have to bite me so damn hard."

CHAPTER EIGHT

MELANY

My heart still pounded in my chest as I stared Lucian in the face. I had to take in a big breath to try and calm down. My flight or fight instincts had kicked in, and unlucky for him I was a fighter. "Why did you grab me?"

Rubbing at his hand, I noticed a red mark on his palm where my teeth had sank in. He shrugged. "I don't know. I saw you sneaking around and thought I'd surprise you."

"Well, you deserved that bite."

His eyes narrowed. "What were you doing, anyway?"

"Nothing."

"Were you coming from the forge?" He peered around the corner at the winding staircase.

"No." I started walking to the dining hall, hoping our conversation was over, but he got in step with me. My stomach growled in reminder I hadn't eaten since breakfast, which was a bowl of oatmeal and an apple.

"You know, I can't figure you out, Blue."

"I didn't realize I was a math equation."

He laughed. "That's what I'm talking about. That surly attitude."

"You know what I think? You're not used to girls with brains. You like girls who fawn at your every word. Girls who swoon when you flex your biceps."

He flexed his arm. "I think it's pretty impressive."

I hated that it was impressive and wouldn't mind wrapping a hand over it. But I wasn't about to let him know that. I knew boys like Lucian. I'd seen them sniffing around Callie. One had sniffed around me once, thinking he could take advantage of the poor girl who lived in the housekeeper's cottage. That boy ended up with a broken nose and ice on his junk after I set him straight and taught him some manners and how consent actually worked.

When we reached the dining hall, I quickly spotted Jasmine and Georgina and fully intended to go sit with them and eat some pizza where it was safe. Standing here next to Lucian felt dangerous. We weren't touching, but I wanted us to. I hated that I thought about his full, soft-looking lips, and how they would feel on mine.

He leaned into me, taking advantage of our height difference. Did he know what I was thinking? The gleam in his eyes worried me. "You look like you want to jump out of your skin."

I licked my lips. "I'm just hungry. I look edgy when I'm hungry."

"I think I make you nervous."

I met his gaze head on. His green eyes had pretty gold flecks in them. "No. Why would you?"

His eyes traveled my face, lingering a bit too long on my mouth. "No reason. I look forward to our next sparring class." He tipped his head and walked into the dining hall to join his friends, who stared our way. I could just imagine what Revana was going to say to him about talking to me.

I quickly made my way to where Jasmine and Georgina sat. Both of them had lifted eyebrows when I sat down and grabbed the piece of pizza they'd gotten for me.

"What was that all about?" Jasmine asked.

"Nothing."

"You know, I think maybe you and I have a very different definition of nothing."

I shoved the pizza in my mouth, ending the conversation about Lucian. I didn't want to talk about him because there *was* something between us. Some kind of energy that sparked every time he was near. It unnerved me. And I couldn't afford to be unnerved. Now that I knew without a shadow of a doubt that I was supposed to be here, I had to concentrate on being the best. Failure wasn't an option for me.

Elemental class was the one class everyone had been waiting for. Not only was it an opportunity to learn how to control various elements like water and lightning, but it was a chance to impress the God of all Gods: Zeus. Just about everyone I knew hoped they had an affinity to lightning, everyone except Georgina. The only God she wished to impress was Demeter. And it's all she would talk about as we made our way across the courtyard to the huge training facility behind the academy.

"Did you know Demeter invented agriculture? Without her we wouldn't even be able to feed ourselves. We'd still be a bunch of Neanderthals eating meat for every meal."

I just nodded and made agreeing noises, as she listed off all the things that Demeter had done or said or discovered. It was a long list, but we made it to the building by the time she finished. The doors opened, and we all walked into a huge, open-air facility that had been separated into different areas. Some of the areas were raised on platforms connected by metal staircases. In each area, I assumed, stood one of the Gods.

I recognized Zeus, who stood on the highest level, three metal rods erected behind him, and Hephaistos, who stood on a lower level next to a large unlit fire pit.

Georgina grabbed my arm and squealed, "It's Demeter." She gestured to the woman with long, messy dark blonde hair, who sat on a huge rock in the middle of a small garden. She wore a long, gauzy skirt, a band

T-shirt that I think it said Jefferson Airplane, and was shoeless.

The man standing near a small pool of water on the lowest level had to be Poseidon. He had a similar face as Zeus, but his hair was dark brown in short waves. I supposed he would be called ruggedly handsome.

"I wonder who that is?" I gestured to the nearest area shrouded in darkness. Every once in a while, I could see a shimmer of movement.

Jasmine frowned. "Who?"

I pointed to the shadows. "There's someone moving around on that platform."

"You're seeing things, Mel. There's no one there."

I peered into the cloying black and spied eyes staring back at me. A shiver of dread rushed down my back.

"Welcome recruits!" Zeus held out his arms toward us. "Today, you will be working with five different elements. Water, fire, earth, shadow, and of course, lightning." White sparks emitted from his fingertips.

Shadow? My gaze tracked over to that area. Now, a man with long, black hair and pale eyes stood there. He dressed like a Victorian vampire. When he spotted me looking at him, he grinned. Goose bumps popped out all over my arms.

"Break out into five groups, eight or nine in each group."

Of course, Jasmine, Georgina, and I melded together. Mia and Ren joined our group. I locked gazes with Lucian. For a brief moment, I thought he was going to walk over to join our group, and I held my breath. But the moment passed, and he gathered with Diego, Revana, and Isobel, along with some others whose names I didn't know. Eventually, Jasmine's room-mate, Hella, and her friends Marek and Quinn, asked to join with us.

Zeus assigned every group an element to start with. We got water.

Ren was bouncing on his toes when we gathered around the pool. He looked like a kid at Christmas.

"Water is life." Poseidon gestured to the pool. "Our bodies are made of it, seventy percent of the world is covered by it, and without it food would not grow." With his hand hovering over the water, slowly it began to swirl like the tide pool we'd used to come to the academy. Then it spouted out of the pool and touched the palm of his hand. There he held it, this swirling column of water.

"But not only can it give life, it can take it away." With a flick of his hand, the narrow waterspout quickly surged into a huge cyclone that towered over us threat-eningly. "The oceans and seas could rise with five hundred foot waves and drown cities in a matter of minutes." He made a fist, and the water sloshed back into the pool, surging over the edge and splashing our legs. "To control the water is to control life."

He looked at each of us. "Who would like to try first?"

Ren's hand shot up like a rocket. "I would, sir."

For the next half hour, we each tried to manipulate the water with our hands. The only two who got it immediately were Ren and Marek. They both were able to produce tiny cyclones. I could barely make the water ripple.

Next, we moved onto the fire station.

"I'm not going to regale you with some soppy story about how powerful fire is," Hephaistos grumbled. "It speaks for itself." He snapped his fingers over the fire pit, and flames jumped to life.

I immediately stepped closer to it, so I could dry off the bottoms of my pants and shoes.

"If you can control fire, you can raze cities to the ground. You can burn your enemies to ash." The light from the flames glowed in his eyes as he walked around behind us.

Jasmine's eyes widened, and it looked like she was shaking.

"But you can also provide warmth and comfort and even healing." He set his hand on her shoulder, and she immediately relaxed and even smiled. "First, you will learn to control the fire, then I will teach you how to create it. Put your hand up to the flames and call it to you."

I raised my hand toward the fire. The heat from it instantly warmed my palm. It reminded me a little of the sensation I'd received from touching the Shadow-box. Concentrating on the flames, I watched them dance. Smiling, I thought about dancing with them.

"Mel," Jasmine said beside me. "Good Gods."

Frowning, I turned to look at her. "What?"

"Your hand!"

I looked at my hand. Flames had completely encompassed it. My heart leapt into my throat. *Holy shit, I'm burning.* But I didn't feel like I was burning. There wasn't any discomfort, just a warm, soothing heat hovering above my skin. I noticed my pants and shoes were no longer wet.

"Whoa!" I moved my hand back and forth, and the flames flowed with me. It was pretty cool.

I glanced at Hephaistos, and he gave me a quick nod.

I figured it was the most praise I was going to get from him. I'd take it.

When we reached the garden, I thought I was going to have to restrain Georgina; she was so excited.

"Controlling the earth is really cool." Demeter climbed off the rock and sat cross-legged on the patch of grass we stood on. She gestured for all of us to sit like she did. "You can grow food and literally move mountains. During war, you can manipulate the plants around you to do whatever you want." She placed her hand flat to the ground, closing her eyes. A vine pushed out of the ground through the grass. It looped around in the air and then wrapped around one of Georgina's arms.

Her eyes widened. She went slack and slumped to the ground.

Demeter frowned. "Shit, man, did I just kill her?"

"No, I think she passed out." I shook Georgina awake.

She sat back up, with a huge smile on her face. "That was awesome."

Everyone laughed.

Demeter chuckled. "What's your name?"

"Georgina," she murmured.

"Well, Georgina, I think you're going to be my fave student."

She nearly passed out again, and I had to hold her up.

Throughout the class, Demeter had us touching the dirt and grass, to really feel it, to think about its construction, and to picture it growing and moving. By the end of the class, Jasmine and Quinn were able to roll a rock without touching it, and Georgina, to the delight of Demeter and everyone else, had grown a flower in her hand. There was no doubt which clan Georgina belonged in.

My group's next stop was at the shadow station. The moment I stepped into the darkness shrouding the area, my body started to vibrate. It was a strange sensation, as if I was a human tuning fork.

"I'm Erebus." From the darkest part of the room, a form stepped into view. Up close, he looked even more like a vampire, especially with those pale, almost translucent eyes. The longer I stared at him, though, the more ethereal he seemed. In fact, his body didn't stay solid. It undulated back and forth. He was part of the shadows.

"Here you will learn how to manipulate light and darkness. When you master it, you will be able to disappear." He faded into the shadows. "And reappear in a different place." His voice came from behind me, and I jumped and whipped around, coming face to face with him. Another rush of dread washed over me.

"I'm going to teach you how to refract light, to bend it around your body. It is a form of disguise, so you can move around without being seen." He put his arms up, slicing them through the air. He did it again and again until they disappeared. "The key is to move quickly. Everyone try it."

As I walked around in a circle, I moved my arms back and forth in front of me, karate chopping the air. I whipped my arms up and down as fast as I could, so focused I almost didn't see Ren as he nearly walked into me.

"Whoa, watch where you're going."

Ren froze. "Melany?"

"Ah, yeah, who else do you think I am?"

His head turned right then left, as if searching for me. "Where are you?"

My brow knitted together. "Right here. In front of you."

He swung around toward me, his eyes darting everywhere, but not on my face. "I can't see you."

Damn. I'd manipulated the light.

"You know, you're quite beautiful."

I whipped around to see Erebus standing behind

me, his hands folded in front of him. "Excuse me? That's a bit creepy, don't you think?"

He took a step closer, his gaze scrutinizing me. I didn't like it. It made me feel vulnerable and exposed.

"You have shadows inside you." He put his hand up and moved it around in front of me. His flesh came apart and then flowed back together. It was like watching an object being refracted into pixels. "I can feel them. It's why you were able to manipulate the light so easily."

"How do I become visible again?"

"Stop moving."

"I'm not moving. I'm just standing here."

He pressed two fingers to my forehead. "Stop moving inside."

I wasn't exactly sure what he meant, but I concentrated on calming my body one part at a time. I started at my toes and made my way up to my head. When I finally took in a long, deep cleansing breath, I felt whole again.

"Dude." Ren's eyes bugged out. "You just appeared in front of me."

Both Jasmine and Georgina ran over to me. "That's so cool. You, like, totally disappeared."

I smiled as they congratulated me. The others gathered around me, too, and told me how awesome it was that I manipulated the light so quickly. No one else had been able to accomplish it. Pride filled me up inside but so did apprehension. I was a bit uneasy with what Erebus had told me—that shadows filled me.

The lightning station with Zeus was our last stop. Jasmine was really pumped for this training. Earlier she'd told me she hoped to be assigned to Zeus's clan. I could see her there; she was strong and bold, two traits of someone who could manipulate lightning.

Zeus had us gathering around what I assumed were lightning rods. The Demos Estate had one on the grounds to try and harness the electrical current whenever it stormed.

"Lightning is just an electrical current," he said, from his spot in the middle of the three rods. "It's in the air all around us, all the time." He clapped his hands together. The sound made everyone jump. He started to rub his palms together. "Rub your hands together. You are creating an electrical charge between them by creating friction."

I could feel heat building between my hands. My fingers started to tingle. I frowned, unsure if that was what was supposed to happen.

While he kept rubbing his hands together, he walked around the group. Then he stopped in front of me, opened his hands, and set them over my head. "We've now created static electricity."

I could feel some slight tingles above me, and then I felt my hair rise. Strands of blue stuck out all over, some of them reaching for Zeus's hands. Both Jasmine and Georgina laughed, as I became a human Troll Doll.

I smirked, amused by what I could imagine I looked like. Then something felt wrong. The tingles around my head increased. It no longer tickled but started to sting. A thousand pinpricks turned sharper, stronger. Painful.

Jasmine's face turned ashen. Georgina took a step back, her eyes widening.

"What? What's going on?" I demanded, panicking.

I could smell something burning, almost like plastic melting. Then I realized the odor emitted from me. Sparks erupted from my head.

"It's going to kill her!" Jasmine's voice echoed around me.

Then everything went black, as darkness took me under.

CHAPTER NINE

MELANY

*T*he smell of bacon and cheese tickled my nose, and I blinked open my eyes. I was in my bed, facing the wall. I rolled to see Georgina and Jasmine, Georgina sat on her bed, and Jasmine was in the desk chair, both eating bacon cheeseburgers and French fries. Saliva instantly pooled in my mouth.

"Yay, you're finally awake." Georgina put another fry into her mouth and happily chewed.

"What happened?" Slowly, I sat up, but my head ached something awful so I reconsidered it.

"You've been out for about four hours." Jasmine came to my side and helped me sit up. She plumped up the pillows behind me. "The healers checked you out, but said you could rest up here in your room instead of in the infirmary."

Georgina unwrapped another burger. "Are you hungry? Do you want to eat?"

I nodded. I was starving. I took the burger and had a big bite. Once I chewed and swallowed, I looked at my friends. "I'm still a bit fuzzy on what exactly happened. I remember being in elemental class with Zeus—"

"You died." Georgina bolted off her bed and wrapped an arm around me, hugging me tight.

I choked on the next bite of burger.

Jasmine gave Georgina a look. "We weren't supposed to tell her right away."

"I know, I'm sorry."

Scrambling out from Georgina's octopus arms, I got all the way out of bed and stared at my friends. "What do you mean, I died?"

"I guess for some reason, a lot of electricity went through your body and your heart stopped." Jasmine winced. "But Zeus got it started again with a little zap of his finger." She poked me in the chest.

"Well, it took two zaps," Georgina added. "And then it still took a few seconds before you came back."

I gaped at her. I had no idea what to say. What did one say after they'd died and had their heart restarted by a God? "Wow" just didn't seem to cut it.

"I need some air." I headed for the door.

"Do you want us to come with?" Georgina started to follow me.

"No. I just… need a walk and some time to digest what happened."

"Okay." Jasmine squeezed my shoulder. "We'll be here when you get back if you want to talk about it."

I left the room and went down the hall, unsure of exactly where I was going. All I knew was that the air inside the school felt thick and oppressive. Thankfully, I didn't run into anyone as I crossed the front foyer and out the main doors.

The second I was outside I took in a deep breath of air, held it, and then let it out. I repeated the process until I wasn't dizzy anymore. I needed to move. I hadn't been outside much on the grounds, so I didn't know where to go, but I knew there was a maze on the west side. I hopped onto the cobblestone path winding through the grounds and just started walking.

Before I came around the corner of the main academy building, I heard a voice. It sounded tinny and mechanical.

"Meteorologists don't know what to make of the strange weather in Pecunia. In some areas, there have been varying degrees of rain, wind, and hail. There have been some large ocean swells, and some are even saying that there has been high seismic activity where there shouldn't be any."

My immediate thought was of Sophia and if she was safe.

Curious, I came around the corner to see Demeter leaning up against the wall, watching a video on her cell phone, and smoking what smelled like weed. When she spotted me, she quickly pushed a button on the screen and slid the phone in her back pocket.

"Oh, hey, there." She smiled, smoke coming out of her mouth. "It's Melany, right?"

I nodded. "Yup."

She raised the joint in her hand. "You don't mind, do you? I can't smoke inside." She shrugged. "Rules suck sometimes."

I shook my head. "I don't mind."

"Good." She took another hit. "So, how are you feeling? You gave everyone quite the scare." She chuckled. "I don't think any of your fellow recruits saw someone die before."

I rubbed at my chest; it still burned where Zeus had zapped me. I was afraid to look under my shirt in case there was a burn mark. "I feel… okay, I guess."

"You'll be all right. Just give it a few days."

"Right." I gestured to her pocket. "Were you watching the news?"

She made a face. "I know I'm not supposed to have a cell phone, either, but sometimes I hate not knowing what's going on around in the world."

"What were they saying about Pecunia? That's where I'm from."

"Ah, nothing to worry about. Just a rainstorm." She patted me on the shoulder.

"Oh, okay." But I wasn't assured.

She took another puff and eyed me. "You're different, you know?"

"What do you mean?"

"Your aura. It's odd. It's not like the others."

I wasn't sure if that was a good thing or a bad

thing. I didn't want to be an outcast. I needed to be like the others, so I could pass through the training.

"It's good being different," she said. "Being like everyone else sucks. Embrace your differences. It'll help you survive."

I was about to say goodnight to her when someone else came stumbling toward us from around the corner. It was Dionysus, and he could barely stay upright. When he saw us, his smile was instant and took up his entire face.

"Heeeeeeeeyyyyy." He weaved toward Demeter and swung an arm around her shoulders. "What are you doing out here, Demi?"

"Just having a smoke. Talking to Melany."

He swung his head my way. "Hello, Melany." He drew out every consonant in my name. "Your aura is funny. It's black."

"She died today."

His eyes bugged out. "You did? How marvelous. What was it like?"

"Um, I don't really remember it."

He scrunched up his face. "Pity. I would've loved to hear all about it." He crushed Demeter to his body. "Let's go party. I made the most amazing hooch."

"Last time I drank your hooch, I had a rash for two weeks."

"No, this batch is good. Trust me. I already drank half of it and I'm fiiiine."

Demeter looked at me. "I'm going to take this one back to his place, so he can sleep it off. You should probably get back to your dorm before curfew. Oh, and I'd really appreciate it if you kept all this to yourself."

"Yeah, no problem. Good night." I turned to go back to the main doors, when Dionysus grabbed my arm.

"Aren't you coming with us, luv?"

Demeter pulled him away. "She can't come with us. She's a first year recruit and has to get back to her dorm."

He nodded. "Riiiiiiiight. I knew that."

They started to walk away when Dionysus swung back around toward me. "I know what it is about you. Your tattoos are dancing."

"I think it's just your eyes, Dion." Demeter waved at me to continue on, as she guided Dionysus around to the back of the school.

Freaked out by the encounter, I ran back to the main doors. There was something about the way Dionysus looked at me that made me uneasy. Not like he was creeping on me or anything, but he saw something odd about me. Both Demeter and Dionysus spotted something different about my aura. I didn't know much about auras, but I knew everyone had one, and different colors had different meaning.

I knew red indicated love and compassion and sometimes anger, yellow meant optimism and intelligence, green meant balance and nature, white, of course, indicated truth and purity. But black, black was not a color a person wanted in their aura. It could mean lots of things like pent up anger and grief, maybe some health problems. And death. Black was the color of shadow and darkness and the eternal abyss.

I hoped it was because I'd died but had come back, and whatever energy required for my resurrection still lingered over me. And not because Death hadn't finished what he'd started.

Once inside the academy, I dashed up the stone staircase and down the long corridor toward the dorm. The lights along the wall appeared dimmer. Every one of them flickered as I passed by. Darkness seemed to be growing along the floor and up the walls. I heard whispering from the shadows.

I stopped and peered into the darkened corners. "Are you playing some kind of game, Erebus? You're wasting your time if you are." A shiver rushed down my back.

A form flickered in the shadows. Someone was moving inside the darkness. I took a step closer. "I can see you. You're not scaring me."

More whispers sounded in my ears, prickling the back of my neck. I spun around, expecting someone to be standing behind me, but there wasn't anyone. I was still alone in the corridor. Except I didn't feel alone. I was being watched.

I turned back to the deep shadows along the wall and swore they had swelled farther along the ceiling and the floor. It was like a slicker of oil slowly rolling toward my shoes. A voice in my head told me to run, but there was also another presence urging me to step into the darkness.

Like a siren's song, I felt compelled to move forward. I stared even harder into the shadows, seeing a face forming from the ink. It was a nice face, a welcoming one. I smiled. Then I lifted my leg to take that step.

"Mel?"

I felt a tug on my hand.

"It's curfew. We need to get to our room."

There was another tug on my hand, and I was suddenly moving sideways.

The spell broke, and I turned to see Georgina leading me back to our room. Before she yanked me inside, I looked over at the shadows once more, and spotted a form standing in the dark, and he was smiling back at me.

CHAPTER TEN

MELANY

*T*he next few weeks just floated by in a bit of a fuzzy haze. Ever since the accident in elemental class and the strange occurrence in the hallway, I'd felt different. Something had changed inside me, and I wasn't sure what it was. The one thing I did notice was that some of the classes became easier.

I no longer missed the targets in archery. In fact, I hit the bullseyes often now, to the delight of Artemis and chagrin of Revana. She'd made her loathing of me known on more than one occasion, especially if I excelled at something she didn't.

And I was getting the hang of metallurgy. It helped that I seemed to have an affinity to fire, which had showed itself in elemental class before I got electrocuted and died. The shield I was crafting in class looked the best out of the entire first years. Hephaistos had even gifted me with some praise in the form of a few non-guttural grunts and a hearty slap on the back that nearly toppled me over.

Spears and shield class still proved difficult, but I think it had more to do with the fact that Ares seemed to have it in for me. He took great pleasure whenever I failed at something. I'd gotten stronger, though, so holding up the shield was a lot easier, and I was decent protecting myself with it. I still struggled a little with holding and maneuvering the spear. I suspected I was going to be much better at handling a sword, and was eager to prove that theory when we had swordplay class next term.

I also saw a jump in improvement with hand-to-hand combat training. Lucian had mentioned it during one class right after I flipped him over onto his back in one quick move that he hadn't seen coming. Heracles had laughed with delight after that, which embarrassed Lucian. His cheeks had flared red.

I thought for sure he'd be all sulky after that and maybe even be a jerk to me, as most boys would after being bested by a girl, but to my surprise and pleasure, he asked me to show him how to do the move. We even practiced it a few times after class until Heracles kicked us out.

During that time, I'd been ultra-aware of every-thing about Lucian, especially when our bodies pressed against each other during the actual flip, and after when he wouldn't release my wrist right away. His touch continually made my body tingle and my head fuzzy, which was why I avoided him at all costs outside of the classroom.

When we weren't in classes, Georgina, Jasmine, and I spent our time together either in our rooms eating and playing cards, or down in the common room where once or twice Dionysus would show up with some new song he created and make us listen to it on repeat. Those were fun nights and made me forget about the odd sensation growing inside of me. Every now and then, I'd catch Dionysus looking at me funny, and I wondered if he still saw my tattoos dancing and a dark aura hovering around me. I never asked, though. I was too afraid to.

I yawned again, as we made our way through the academy to the Hall of Aphrodite for our transformation class. The word was that the Goddess never left her gilded hall. I knew that was a lie, as I'd seen her skulking around with Ares on my first night at the academy. But I kept that information to myself.

"Are you still not sleeping?" Georgina gave me a concerned look.

"I'm fine. Just woke up a little earlier than I wanted."

She didn't look convinced.

I'd woken up at three o'clock, again for the fifth day in a row. I had a feeling I was having bad dreams, but I couldn't remember them when I woke. All that lingered was a feeling of ominous dread. So, it proved difficult to get back to sleep after waking. Some mornings I would just lie there in bed, staring at the ceiling, so I didn't wake Georgina. Other times, I walked the dark hallways of the academy, and made it a game of not getting caught by the hall monitors. Pandora had almost busted me the other morning, but I'd managed to duck into the girls' shower room before she could spot me. I figured I was improving my stealth skills.

It was my first time in the Hall of Aphrodite, so I didn't know what to expect. I'd heard a few of the first years, like Revana and Lucian, had been invited for a private dinner party a week ago by Eros and Psyche to the hall. It bothered me that even here, money and power and good looks gave you advantages the rest of us didn't have. After reading about Aphrodite over the years and overhearing some of the other recruits talking about it, I expected splendor. The reality of the hall far surpassed anything I could ever imagine.

The floor was a labyrinth of gold and red and black tile, producing an optical illusion of boxes stacked on top of one another. It was polished to a shine, and I could see my reflection in it as clear as a mirror. The arched ceiling was embossed with gold and painted with frescos done in red and gold and of Aphrodite and her various companions like Eros, her son, and the three Graces—Aglaia, Euphrosyne, and Thalia. Everywhere you looked, there were carved pillars holding up the ceiling, also gold embossed, and the walls were wallpapered in red velvet. I'd never seen anything so gauche; it nearly hurt my eyes.

As a group, we entered the adjacent room to the

lavish front entrance of the hall, which I assumed was the classroom. Thankfully, it wasn't as opulently decorated. I didn't think I could've handled all that gold and red for two hours. Fifty high-backed chairs were arranged around a raised pulpit. It reminded me of a church. The Church of Aphrodite.

While we all got seated—Jasmine, Georgina, and I sat together as usual—the door at the back of the room opened, and Aphrodite walked in, head high, breasts jutted, hips swaying. She was accompanied by three other women, two of them carried the train on her lavish gold gown, and the other carried a large, black leather case.

Everyone was transfixed as she stepped up onto the pulpit, especially the boys. I didn't blame them; she was stunning up close. It was almost difficult to look upon her, like looking into the hottest part of the sun. She was too bright.

She waited until she had everyone's rapt attention before she spoke. "Transformation. It is the act of changing into something else. A caterpillar into a butterfly." Her gaze swept the audience. "A tadpole into a frog. I will teach you how to change your look, your shape, so you can turn into someone else. It is a masterful skill to have in order to deceive your enemies or to even hide among them." She looked right at me.

For the next two hours, Aphrodite showed us how to alter the shape of our faces, which was the first step to transformation. At first I couldn't believe it was even possible, but after she demonstrated by changing her appearance into that of an old, withered hunchback hag, I became a true believer.

With the help of her assistants, who ended up being the three Graces, Aglaia, Euphrosyne, and Thalia, we each took turns either plumping up our faces or thinning them down. Georgina, Jasmine, and I couldn't stop giggling, as Georgina ended up fattening her face so much she looked like a tomato, especially with her red hair. By the end of the class, it was obvious she had a knack for changing. Jasmine and I didn't latch onto it as well. I think all I managed to do was to make my nose long and thin like Pinocchio, which made everyone around us laugh hysterically. Lucian included.

At the end of class, I was leaving with my friends when Aphrodite called me back.

"Melany, why don't you stay a minute?"

Both Georgina and Jasmine gave me funny looks. I shrugged and then walked back to where the Goddess stood waiting. "Did I do something wrong?"

She gave me an indulgent smile, but it didn't make me feel warm. A shiver actually rushed down my back. "On the contrary, I've only heard great things about you."

I grimaced. "Really?"

"Oh yes, you have made quite a stir around the academy."

She was probably referring to the incident in elemental class when I'd gotten electrocuted. Despite that, I was still surprised Aphrodite even knew my name. She didn't seem like the sort of person who even bothered with that trivial information.

"My husband talks quite fondly of you."

Now, I really did give her a look. There was no way Hephaistos said anything complimentary about me to his wife. He wouldn't say anything nice like that to anyone. Maybe she heard from her lover, Ares, about what a pain in the ass I was.

"And because of that, I want you to know, that if you ever need someone to talk to, you can come to me." Her gaze scrutinized me from toe to head. "I can imagine it must be hard for you here, considering you're... so different from everyone else."

I wondered if she meant my strange aura, or if she meant that I had blue hair, piercings, and tattoos, and didn't look as pampered and polished as everyone else, especially Revana and her crew.

"I, ah, appreciate that." I wasn't sure what else to say. As if I would confide in her, knowing full well that she was conspiring with Ares about something. Although she was breathtaking, there was something utterly deceptive about her. Maybe it was the fact that she could transform into anyone. If that wasn't the ultimate trickery, I didn't know what was.

She set her hand on my arm, and I felt a prickle of heat along my skin. "I was very concerned when I heard what had transpired in your elemental training. Zeus's lightning is very dangerous. I've told him time and time again that he shouldn't be teaching that so soon in a young one's training. Disastrous accidents can happen. Obviously." Her hand stayed on my arm, and my head started to feel a bit floaty. Like I'd drunk too much wine. "Do you remember anything about how you survived? Did someone help you?"

I frowned. "Zeus brought me back."

"That's not how I understand it. He said he tried to bring you back, but it didn't work."

I wanted to pull away from her. My face was flushed, and too much heat circulated in my body. I felt drunk. But not just on alcohol—on her. She smelled like wild flowers, and her hair was so shiny and soft looking, I wanted to reach out and twirl a tendril of it on my finger, like spinning gold.

"Can you remember who brought you back? Did someone whisper to you?"

I shook my head, trying to clear it. Her words were like a lullaby in my ears, lulling me into a daze. Seducing me into submission.

Fight her.

I heard the voice in my head. It was like the whispers I'd heard before. From the shadows. In my dreams.

Her hand tightened on my arm, like a snake. Constricting me. "Tell me what you know. Tell me—"

With everything I had, I pushed her away, both physically and mentally. I stumbled backwards and nearly fell onto my ass. I expected anger from her for assaulting her. But she just smiled, as if nothing had happened.

"You should run along my dear. Your friends will be

missing you." Her grin widened. It almost appeared as if her teeth had sharpened, but that could've been my imagination. "Won't they?"

Without responding, I turned and ran out of the room then out of the hall. The big, heavy gold doors slammed shut behind me the second I was out. The sudden need to be with my friends spurred me on, and I ran through the academy halls to the dorms.

I didn't quite know what had just happened with Aphrodite, but a sense of dread tightened in my guts. I'd been in danger that much I grasped, but I didn't know why. How was I a threat to Aphrodite? And what was she willing to do to end it?

CHAPTER ELEVEN

MELANY

*P*itch black surrounded me. I felt like I was floating. I could see a pinpoint of light, and that was when I realized I was back inside the spiraling portal underwater. My lungs burned from lack of oxygen. A few more minutes and I would certainly die.

I looked past the portal to the dark waters beyond, and saw a shape hovering nearby. Watching me. I reached out toward the form, pleading for help. Suddenly I didn't know how to swim. I didn't know why I was here in this portal again, but I was going to die if I didn't get out.

My fingers breached the edge of the whirling spout. My hand reached for the form floating within inches of me. I wriggled my fingers, grasping for assistance. *"Help me!"* I tried to scream, but when I opened my mouth, water poured in. And now, I was choking on it.

My vision blurred. The pressure inside my head expanded. Pain pummeled at me. It wouldn't be long before I succumbed to the water and took it in.

Then a hand snatched mine and pulled me out.

Bolting straight up in bed, I coughed and sputtered, taking in greedy gulps of air. Whispers swirled around me, trying to penetrate my ears. But I didn't want to listen to them. They were telling me bad things. Asking me to do bad things.

I swatted at them, buzzing like stinging insects. "Stop it!"

Then I felt warm hands on top of mine. "Mel! You're okay. You're safe."

Slowly, my surroundings came into view. I was in my bed, in my dorm. And Georgina held me, talking me out of whatever fugue I'd been trapped inside.

She ran a hand over my head. "You're okay. You're here, with me."

I nodded, and took in a deep breath, trying to slow my heart rate, which thundered in my chest, each beat like a hammer against my rib cage.

"Same dream?" she asked.

I nodded.

For the past nine days, I'd been having the same horrible dream every night. It all started right after the incident with Aphrodite. It was almost like she'd sparked something inside me. Tried to force open some door inside my mind. And it was opening. I could hear it creaking inside my head and feel every small progression in my body. I feared what was inside.

After Georgina helped me calm down, we dressed and headed to the dining hall for breakfast. Jasmine caught up with us, and upon seeing me, immediately hugged me.

"Are you okay? You look so pale."

I gave her a look.

"Well, paler than usual."

"Bad dreams still," Georgina piped up, as she slopped oatmeal into a bowl and handed it to me.

We took our meals and sat at our usual spot at one of the long tables in the hall. Mia joined us, and I noticed the instant grin on Jasmine's face.

"Are they the same?" Jasmine asked.

"Yeah, I'm trapped in the portal underwater, and I'm going to drown, but someone who I can't see pulls me out right before." I played with my oatmeal, not hungry at all.

"Maybe it's just stress getting the best of you," Jasmine said. "That is sort of what happened to you getting here, wasn't it? I mean, Lucian saved you, didn't he?"

I nodded, just as my gaze landed on him two tables away, laughing with his friends. He glanced up from his meal and caught me looking at him. Before I could turn away, he gave me a soft smile that made my heart thump a little bit faster.

"Maybe you're stressed about the practice water trial today." Mia shrugged.

Georgina nodded. "I bet that's it. You did tell me you weren't looking forward to it since you didn't do too well in water."

"Yeah, you're probably right." I smiled at my friends, knowing they all meant well and were only looking out for me. But they were wrong in this. It wasn't stress trying to burrow into my mind like a worm in dirt; it was something altogether more worrisome. Something sinister.

There was a buzz of excitement and apprehension during elemental class. After our lessons with the other elements, we were all going to be doing a practice water trial in the pool with Poseidon. Despite my attempts to deny it to myself, I was nervous about the trial. I wasn't all that good with water or in it. After six classes, I'd only been able to make a tiny cyclone in the water while some like Ren, Marek, and even Lucian, could make waves as high as the twenty foot ceiling. But the prep training wasn't about making water spouts and waves, it was about staying underwater for as long as possible and collecting rocks from the bottom of the pool. It seemed simple enough, but the catch was we had to do it while evading an attack from some water beast Poseidon was going to set loose. *Fun times at Poseidon's pool party.*

The whole thing was a distraction, and I nearly set Hella's pants on fire when a fireball I was making got away from me, bounced once, and exploded at her feet. Hephaistos rushed over with a bucket of water and doused her before it could do any damage.

"I'm so sorry." I rushed over to her, my hands still aflame.

"It's fine." She moved away from me.

But I could see it in her face that it was far from fine, and now she was afraid of me. I supposed I didn't blame her; I had come at her waving around my fire hands.

"What's wrong with you, girl?" Hephaistos growled at me, tossing the rest of the water from the bucket onto me to douse my hands. "You have to stay focused, or you're going to hurt someone."

That distraction followed me through shadow class, as I walked through the motions, dissipating at will, then to lightning where I was barely even allowed to touch the metal rods in case I got electrocuted again, then over to the garden, where we were practicing growing vines. I hadn't managed to do anything in this class. I knew it wasn't possible to be good at everything, but I had no affinity to the earth and plants whatsoever. The rest of my group had been able to at least coax a flower to open its petals and to move a huge boulder across the garden. Georgina was already growing fruits and vegetables with the touch of her hands and the intention in her heart.

After having completely given up, I sat on the ground and watched as the others tried to coax some vines to wrap around Demeter's legs. I laughed when Jasmine's vine went crazy and did a loop around her feet and tried to trip her.

I heard other laughter, and my gaze drifted over to

where Lucian and his group were at the fire station. Revana and Isobel were huddled together, looking my way and snickering. When Revana spotted me watching them, she sneered.

I didn't know how one person could be so hateful. It wasn't just me who she looked down on, either; it was almost everyone except her immediate friends, although I had overheard her talking crap about Isobel behind her back to Diego.

As I stared at her, I got angrier and angrier. Gritting my teeth and pressing my hands down into the dirt, I thought someone needed to shut her up. She reminded me so much of Callie with her backhanded remarks, disdainful looks, and condescending manner. I'd put up with it for years, swallowing it down over the lump in my throat because I hadn't had a choice.

While Revana continued to smirk and sneer, probably remarking about how trashy I was, all I could picture was a gag in her mouth. It was such a vivid image that I grinned.

Then I was being shaken out of my stupor. "Snap out of it, Melany."

I looked up as Demeter squeezed my shoulder. "What? What's going on?"

"Let go of Revana."

I frowned, confused. My gaze swung over to the fire station and I gasped.

Revana had vines wrapped around her head, over her mouth in particular. Every time she struggled, the vines seemed to be pulling even tighter until her eyes bugged out. Then I noticed the vine had originated from a plant near my shoe. I jumped to my feet, and immediately the vine went slack, and she and Isobel were able to tear it off her face.

The second she was freed, Revana came at me like a freight train. "You bitch."

I managed to dodge her first punch before Demeter intervened.

"Enough."

"She tried to kill me!"

Demeter made a face. "I'm sure that's not true. It was totally an accident, wasn't it, Melany?"

I nodded.

Zeus peered down at us from overhead. "Everything all right down there?"

"Yup, just a little mishap." Demeter gave him the thumbs up. "Nothing to worry about."

"Should we discuss it in council chambers later this evening?" He narrowed his eyes at me.

Demeter shook her head. "No, I don't think that needs to happen." She glanced at Revana. "No one's hurt. Right?"

Revana glared at me but shook her head.

"You see, it's all good."

"Return to your training." Zeus turned and gestured to his class, who were all peering over the side.

Revana, accompanied by Isobel, returned to the fire station. Everyone else went back to what they were doing before chaos had ensued. Demeter put her hand on my shoulder.

"Where did that come from?"

I shook my head. "I don't know. I was just sitting there."

"Something happened."

"I got angry I think."

She nodded. "I have to say I've never seen anyone in all my years of teaching do that at this level." She winked and patted my shoulder. "Well done."

Finished at the other elemental stations, we all gathered around the pool to wait for instructions from Poseidon. The other professors had joined us as well to watch. Nerves zipped through me, and I couldn't stop fidgeting.

"The object of this exercise"—Poseidon leisurely walked behind us, handing each of us a small mesh bag —"is to stay underwater and collect as many rocks as you can. Sounds easy enough. Except for one thing… you will have to evade my adorable pet Charybdis." He pointed to the water.

I gazed down into the pool to see a three-foot long, serpent-like creature whipping around in the water. I'd never seen a Charybdis in person, but the rumor was they possessed nine eyes that circled a round mouth lined with razor sharp teeth. I swallowed the bile rising in my throat.

"Don't worry, a bite from a baby Charybdis isn't lethal, but it does sting a bit." He grinned. "The prize for gathering twenty or more rocks is the favor of the Gods, and you will enjoy a lavish dinner in Zeus's Great Hall with me and Zeus himself."

I saw a lot of excited faces at that prospect. I wasn't one of them.

"BEGIN!"

One by one, my fellow recruits dove into the pool. I watched them go under, frozen in spot, completely petrified, the images and sensations of my dreams holding me hostage. I couldn't do it. I couldn't jump in.

Then Poseidon shoved me in from behind.

As I plunged under the water, I nearly collided with Jasmine, as she grabbed a couple rocks and put them into her mesh bag. When she saw me, she gave me a thumbs up and pointed to the rocks. I nodded and kicked my legs to dive to the bottom.

I scooped up a handful and put them in my bag. Movement next to me drew my attention. I looked up just in time to get Revana's fist in my face. The viscosity of the water softened the blow, or I was sure that it would've knocked me out. Blood floated in front of my eyes. It was coming from my nose.

She reared back to hit me again, when Lucian swam in between us. He shook his head at her, pointing for her to go. She did, but reluctantly. When she was gone, he swirled around to me, pointed at me, then gave the okay sign.

I nodded to let him know I was fine. Smiling, he scooped up a couple more rocks and put them in my bag. I shook my head at him but couldn't stop the grin on my face. My stomach lurched, and my grin faded in an instant when I spotted the Charybdis swimming right toward us. It must've been attracted to my blood.

I shoved Lucian to the side just as the creature lunged. I kicked up with my legs, giving me leverage, and punched it right under its mouth. My stomach churned at the feeling of its fleshy mass on my skin. But it did the trick and it scuttled away.

Lucian looked wide-eyed at me. I gave the okay signal and pointed at him. He nodded. Together, we gathered more rocks. I looked around and noticed there were only about five others in the water with me and Lucian. Ren, of course, and Marek, Revana, and two others I didn't know well.

After another minute, my lungs started to burn. The incident with Revana had distracted me, but now that I was floating here, I was reminded of being back in the portal and not being able to breathe. Noticing my rising panic, Lucian swam close and grabbed my hand. It helped calm me down a little.

After another minute, one of the others kicked to the surface. Then Revana looked over at us, and I could see the anger on her face. She struggled to stay under. She started to thrash around, as I imagined the urge to open her mouth pounded at her. She flipped me the middle finger and then kicked hard up to the surface.

I, too, began to struggle. My head grew fuzzy. Black spots started to form in my vision. Then the whispers infiltrated the back of my mind.

Don't be afraid. Let go of the panic. You won't drown. I won't let you.

I didn't know who was talking to me but I listened.

Lucian eventually let go of my hand, kicking up to the surface. Then Marek went up, and then the other girl who I didn't know. It was just Ren and I left. When he noticed, he swam over to me, smiling.

We happily floated in the water together. My lungs started to burn again, but Ren looked like he could stay down here forever. I wondered if he was half fish. He most definitely had Poseidon's blood swimming through his veins.

Knowing Ren would win the prize, I was more than happy to give up and swim to the surface. I was about to when his face changed and his eyes widened. I could sense movement behind me. I spun around to see the Charybdis's mouth just about to clamp down on my head.

CHAPTER TWELVE

LUCIAN

J paced along the edge of the pool, trying hard not jump in, especially after I saw the Charybdis zip through the water toward Melany and Ren.

"She can take care of herself," Poseidon said at my distress.

Everyone watched the pool, waiting to see what would happen. Some were scared, like Melany's friends, Georgina and Jasmine, others, like Revana, looked on in glee, hoping for a lethal outcome.

I watched, my heart in my throat, at the erratic movement in the water, and then the Charybdis came shooting out like a cannon and landed at Poseidon's feet. The little creature looked unharmed, but definitely indignant at being tossed out of the pool.

Laughing, Poseidon picked up the sea slug and patted its head. A few moments later, Melany and Ren popped up out of the water to a round of cheers and clapping.

"Well done, you two are the winners of the competition."

I reached down and helped Ren out of the pool and then Melany. She was shivering, and I draped a big towel around her shoulders. There was still a trickle of blood coming from her nose.

"You still got a bit of blood." I gestured to her nose.

She pressed the edge of her towel to her face. "Thanks."

"Does it hurt?"

"Nah. She punches like a girl."

I laughed, which earned me a lethal glare from Revana, who was chatting with Isobel nearby.

"You should have seen her." Ren was talking to Poseidon and the others who gathered around. "She just reached out and grabbed that thing by the neck before it could bite her and just tossed it through the water like a missile. I've never seen anything like it." He chuckled.

"I don't think it was as cool as that." Melany rubbed at her hair with the towel.

"Oh, yeah it was." Grinning, Ren patted her on the shoulder. "You're hardcore."

Her cheeks flushed a little at the compliment, but I had to agree. Melany was hardcore. She'd saved me from getting bitten by that creepy water slug. And she was consistently kicking my ass in hand-to-hand combat training.

"He's right, Blue." I leaned down to her ear, as we all left the training facility. "You are a badass."

She gave me a look, and I thought she was going to say something, but her friends came up on her sides, pushing me out. I stepped away and joined Diego, Jonah, and Trevin; they were congratulating Ren for winning the competition and basically for being part fish.

Back at the dorms, I'd finished having a shower and was changing into regular clothes since classes were done for the day. I was anxious to get down to the dining hall and chill out. I was hungry, but I also realized it was because I wanted to see Melany. I didn't get a chance to thank her for saving me from getting bitten by the Charybdis, and I just wanted to hang out with her. I didn't know anything about her and I wanted to.

"Can you believe that bitch today?" Diego ran product into his hair. "I mean, Revana should've really kicked her ass."

"Don't talk about her like that." I pulled on my T-shirt.

Diego smirked. "Why are you sticking up for her? Revana's supposed to be your friend."

"She is, but sometimes she gets what she asks for."

"What is that supposed to mean?"

"She's not always a nice person." I sat on my bed to put on my shoes.

"Nice is overrated," Diego said. "It's not going to

get you anywhere in this place." He frowned at me. "And since when were you nice to girls like Melany?"

I shrugged. "She's different. I like her."

"I'd like her, too, if she put out." He made a rude gesture with his hips.

"Don't be an asshole."

I left the room without him. Diego and I had been friends before the academy, same with Revana. We all ran in the same affluent circles. We were all from devout families, who had started our training when we were young. Someone in each of our families had been called to the army in the past. For me, it was my brother, Owen. Diego's uncle from Argentina had been called thirty years ago. Revana's patronage was even older—her maternal grandfather had gotten the invitation mere months after her mother had been born. So, I basically grew up around them, but I was starting to realize that neither of them were good people. If we hadn't known each other before, I wasn't sure I'd go out of my way to know them now.

I hurried to the dining hall, grabbed some food, and sat at a table near the main doors. I wanted to see when Melany came in. Soon, Diego and the others joined me.

"Why are you sitting here?" Revana set her tray down beside mine.

"Change of pace." Taking my eyes off the main door, I shoveled some food into my mouth.

Isobel stole a fry from Diego's tray. "I think it was

totally unfair Melany won along with Ren. It should've just been Ren."

"She must've cheated," Revana said. "She hasn't shown an affinity to water at all over the past few weeks. Last time, she couldn't even make a spout."

I sniffed and shook my head. "She didn't cheat."

She gave me a haughty look. "How do you know?"

"Because I was down there with her, and she was just better than everyone else. Me included."

Frowning, she turned to talk to Isobel, who was busy eating all the fries from Diego's tray. I didn't think he minded, though, because I was pretty sure he was crushing hard on her. He always looked at her like a clueless puppy.

"Hey, did you guys hear about New Athens, Kios, and Pecunia?" Trevin asked. "Supposedly, there have been some earthquakes around there."

"Where did you hear that?" Jonah frowned. I could hear the concern in his voice.

"Are you from there?" I asked.

"Around there. I'm from the town over, Histria."

"Someone snuck a cell phone in," Trevin said. "It's all over the news."

"Sounds like a bad rumor to me. No one would be able to sneak a phone in. No way," Isobel said. "Besides, they'd tell us if something like that happened to where we're from." She looked around at everyone. "Wouldn't they?"

"Of course they would." Revana patted Isobel's hand. The girl looked like she was about to cry.

When I spotted Georgina and Jasmine entering the dining hall, I got to my feet. "I'll catch up with you guys later."

"Where are you going?" Revana called after me.

I didn't stop until I reached Georgina and Jasmine. Surprise flashed across both their faces at seeing me at their table. I slid in beside Jasmine.

"What do you want?" she asked.

"Where's Blue?"

Georgina's eyebrows shot up. "She's back in the dorm, resting. The whole thing in the pool took its toll on her."

"What do you want with her?" Jasmine gave me a pointed look, which I didn't blame her for. I hadn't been the friendliest person over the last month or so.

"Nothing. I just want to see if she's okay."

"She's fine." Jasmine went back to her food and talking to Mia, who sat on her other side.

I guessed that was the end of that conversation.

I got up from the table, but I didn't want to go back and sit with Diego and the others, and I didn't want to return to my dorm room. I wanted to see Melany. After I did a drive by the food line and grabbed a couple of chocolate cupcakes, I headed out of the dining hall and toward the girls' dorm.

I didn't know how I was going to get past the dorm monitor, but I was going to give it a go. What was the worst that could happen?

I ran up the stairs and turned left toward the girls' dorm rooms. Before I entered the main corridor, I stopped and peered around the corner, planning my strategy. I could dissipate into the shadows like Erebus had taught us. I wasn't great at it, not like Melany, but I had improved. I just needed more shadows to move through; there was too much light in the hall.

I looked around on the ground and spied a small pebble. I picked it up, rubbing it between my fingers, gauging my aim at the light in the sconce along the wall. Taking a deep breath, I reared back and threw the rock. Like a targeted missile, it hit the light and broke the bulb. Shadows instantly filled that side of the corridor.

Before anyone could come investigate the sound, I streaked down the hallway, keeping to the darkness hugging the far wall. I concentrated on refracting the light, so if anyone peered out from one of the rooms, they wouldn't see me, not unless they really stared into the shadows hard, then they'd probably see some movement.

As I made my way through the dorm, I realized I had no idea which room was Melany's. All I knew was that she bunked with Georgina. But I did remember one time when Georgina mentioned that they were always the last ones out of the dorm in the morning. So I assumed they were one of the last rooms.

At the end of the hall, there were two rooms; one had the door open, and it was dark inside, and the other's door was shut, light spilling from underneath, and the sounds of some kind of thrash metal emanated from within. This had to be Melany's room. She was the only girl I knew who would listen to thrash metal.

I knocked on the door and waited, feeling nervous all of a sudden.

The door swung open to a scowly face. "What?" Then her eyes widened.

I held out my hand, a chocolate cupcake balanced on the palm. "I come bearing gifts."

She took a step out and glanced down the corridor. "What are you doing here?"

"I heard you weren't feeling all that well, so I thought you might need some sustenance."

She narrowed her eyes. "You know this is weird, right?"

I grimaced. "I guess. But we're at a school for demigods, I think weird is relative at this point."

"Good point." She plucked the cupcake from my hand.

I leaned in the doorway. "Can I come in?"

She opened the door wider and gestured with her arm. I entered, my shirt starting to feel a bit constricting at the collar. I pulled at it and looked around. Everything looked the same as my dorm room. I wasn't sure what I had expected. Maybe pink wallpaper and furry pillows, although Melany wasn't the pink and furry type at all.

I sat on the floor; I didn't want to be presumptuous and sit on her bed. She joined me, sitting cross-legged. She peeled off the cupcake wrap and took a big bite.

Icing got on the tip of her nose, and I pressed my lips together to stop from laughing.

"What?" She gave me a funny look.

I reached over and wiped the icing off her nose, and then we ate in silence. It was nice to just sit with her and not have to make conversation. When she was done, she licked her fingers clean.

"That was delicious, thanks." She gave me a small smile.

As she fidgeted a bit, I took the moment to take her in. All of her. She was so different than the girls I was used to. The ones who I grew up with were poised and polished, cultured and refined, raised from day one to be a perfect specimen, devout to the Gods, loyal to family. I saw nothing like that in Melany.

I reached over and touched the dark tattoo winding around her arm. "What does this one mean?"

"How do you know it means something?"

"Because you don't seem like a girl who does things senselessly."

"The snake. It means rebirth, an awakening. It reminds me that I can be whatever I want to be. I'm in charge of my destiny."

"Says the girl invited by a mysterious metal box to train in an army for the Gods." I chuckled.

"Hey, I chose to come here. I didn't have to. The invitation is just that, isn't it? An invitation. It's up to every person whether to answer it or not."

I frowned at her. I'd never thought of it that way. Although in my family, there was no question about me coming to the academy. I didn't think I would've been allowed to say no.

I gestured to the others on her arms.

"It's two ravens intertwined. They're for my parents, who died when I was little. Some kind of accident I'm told."

"Oh, I'm sorry."

She shrugged. "It's fine. I was like maybe three or four. I was taken to an orphanage. Bounced around from foster home to foster home, until my mother's estranged sister, Sophia, discovered I existed. She adopted me when I was thirteen."

"That must've been hard."

"It is what it is. I try not to dwell on it." She ran her fingers over the last markings on her forearms. "And the skulls... well, I just think they look cool."

"That they do." I laughed. "What did your adopted mom say about them?"

"She was fine with them. It was the Demos family that hated them."

The name sounded familiar. "The Demos's?"

"Sophia worked for them. We lived on their estate."

"They have a daughter named... Callie, right?"

She gaped. "Yes. You know them?"

I shrugged. "A little. My father knew Mr. Demos. They did some business together."

She shook her head. "Wow. Maybe we crossed paths at one of their huge parties."

"I don't think so. I would've definitely remembered you."

She blushed a little, and I wanted to grab her leg, pull her closer, and kiss her. The urge raced through me like wildfire. I was surprised how potent it was, how potent she was.

Then another thought intruded. Something someone had said earlier in the dining hall.

"You lived in Pecunia?"

She nodded, her brow slowly furrowing. "Why?"

"It's probably nothing. I don't want to worry you."

"Well, you already have, so you might as well tell me."

"There's a rumor going around that Pecunia and a couple other places had an earthquake."

Her face paled, and I thought she was going to pass out.

CHAPTER THIRTEEN

MELANY

"*P*ecunia doesn't have earthquakes." I stared at him, hoping he had misspoke, and he was talking about some other town.

"I'm sure it was just a rumor."

I jumped to my feet, my mind going a mile a minute. All I could think about was if Sophia was safe. Who would be there to protect her if something happened? "You need to tell me everything you heard."

"Trevin said he overheard it from someone who had smuggled a phone in. That it was all over the news that Pecunia, New Athens, and Kios had suffered an earthquake." His brow knitted together. "I'm pretty sure it's not true."

"It's pretty random not to be true, don't you think?" My heart raced. I didn't know what to do, but I had to do something. There had to be a way to confirm the information.

Demeter. She owed me one.

"C'mon." I slid on my boots, heading out the door.

"Where are we going?"

"To find out if it's true or not." I didn't wait for him to respond.

He caught up to me as I pushed through the main doors to the outside and rounded the corner of the building on the cobblestone path. Demeter was exactly where I'd seen her last time, leaning up against the wall and smoking some weed.

She shook her head when she spotted Lucian and I. "Pretty soon, my secret isn't going to be a secret."

"I need your phone."

She made a face. "Any particular reason?"

"I need to see the news."

Her face changed; it was subtle, but I'd seen it in the slight downward tilt of her lips. She knew what I was after.

"Is it true?" I asked her.

She shrugged. "Don't know what you're talking about."

"Look, I know you're a Goddess, and you could smite me in mere seconds, but I'm asking for you to be a human being right now and do me a favor."

I felt Lucian tense beside me. He probably thought I was insane to talk to one of the Gods like this, but I didn't feel like I had a choice.

"Besides, you do owe me one," I said as a last

resort.

Sighing, Demeter reached into her back pants pocket and pulled out her cell phone. She handed it to me.

When I pressed the main button, a news video was paused on the home screen. I pushed play.

"The damage here in Pecunia is devastating. In all my years of news reporting, I have never seen destruction like this…"

The news reporter walked past destroyed buildings, half a cement wall still stood in one lot, debris surrounding it. Behind him downed powerlines sparked. He neared a street sign that was bent in half. I could read the sign though—Homer Avenue. I knew that avenue; I knew that corner block he was moving past. It was just down the hill from the Demos Estate. Callie and I had been there countless times to get iced coffees and cappuccinos.

Lucian set his hand on my arm; he'd been behind me, watching the video over my shoulder. "Are you okay, Blue?"

A sudden coldness hit my core. Was I okay? I didn't know.

I looked over at Demeter; she'd been watching me. "When did this happen?"

"Yesterday."

"Would you have told me? Told any of us?"

She looked me dead in the eyes. "What would have been the point? You can't do anything about it. It would have only interfered with your training."

I slapped the phone back into her hand, uncaring

that she was a powerful being and could destroy me with a blink of her eye. "How do I get out of here?"

She shook her head. "You can't."

"I don't believe that. There has to be a way for us to leave."

"If you leave the academy, you'll be immediately expelled and have your memories erased, and you won't ever be able to go back to your home. You'll become one of the *lost*."

I made a face. "According to the news, I don't have a home to go to, anyway."

"Blue... she's right." Lucian rubbed his hand over my shoulder. "There's nothing—"

I pulled away from him. "I have to go. I have to make sure Sophia is okay. She doesn't have anyone but me." Tears welled in my eyes, but I wouldn't let them fall. I refused to appear weak in front of either of them.

Demeter pushed off the wall, grabbing me by the upper arms. "Listen to me, Melany. There is nothing you can do for her by going to Pecunia. The best thing you can do is to stay here and complete your training. Your training is more important than you can even imagine."

It was obvious she was keeping something to herself. The Gods weren't known for their forthcoming nature.

"Tell me why it's so important, and I'll forget about leaving."

She stared at me for a long moment, then sighed, dropped her hands, and took a step back. She looked at

Lucian. "Talk some sense into your girlfriend." She reached behind her ear, pulled out another joint, and lit it up. "I'd get back into the school before curfew." Puffing, she walked away toward the maze.

I wanted to go after her and demand to know what was going on, but I knew she wouldn't tell me the truth. The Gods worked in mysterious ways, my ass. They were just jerks.

"C'mon, let's go back," Lucian said.

When I didn't walk with him immediately, he grabbed my hand and pulled me with him to the main doors. He opened the door for me and we went inside. He took my hand again and I let him. It felt good to be touching him. It grounded me a little.

As we walked up the stone staircase to the dorms, Lucian stopped and turned me to him. "I might know a way out."

"How?"

"I need to know that you understand the consequences. That it is worth it to you."

"I have to know that Sophia made it out. She sacrificed a lot for me. I need to be willing to do the same for her."

He nodded. "I heard there is a network of deep underground tunnels under the academy leading to the mainland."

"Where's the entrance?"

"In the forge."

I frowned. "You mean in Hephaistos's lair?"

"No, like literally in the mouth of the dragon

forge."

"Through the fire."

He nodded. "Yeah."

"This just gets better and better." I rubbed my hands over my face. "Is this reliable intel? I don't want to be risking everything and find out I'm just going to set myself on fire."

"Dionysus mentioned it one night."

I grimaced. "Dionysus who makes poisonous potions and drinks them to see how they taste? That Dionysus?"

"He mentioned it one night when he was hanging out with some of the guys in our dorm. He told us it's how he gets out to visit his lady friends."

I shook my head.

"Hey, I wouldn't suggest it to you if I thought it wasn't going to work. You have to remember the Gods are trapped here, too. Of course they're going to know secret ways out of here."

"Okay, but I need to talk to him. I need to know exactly how to get out. Do you know where I can find him?"

Lucian shook his head. "I have no idea. He's not—"

Music suddenly blasted from the corridor leading to the great hall.

When we stepped into the hall, we were bombarded with the loudest, most heart-thumping bass. It actually brought tears to my eyes. Dionysus rolled toward us on one of Hephaistos's serving robots.

He was perched on top of it like a crazed vulture with a black Mohawk and black eye-liner running down its face.

"Lucian!" He wheeled around us, laughing manically. "Melany!" He said both our names in long, drawn out syllables.

"I need to ask you something." I had to yell to be heard over the music.

"What?"

"Can you turn down the music, so we can have a conversation?"

"Sure." He snapped his fingers and the music died. "What do you want to talk about?"

"Is there a way out of the academy through the forge?"

His gaze whipped over to Lucian. "I thought we were bros. I told you that in confidence."

"It's important. I had to tell her." Lucian set his hand on my shoulder in solidarity.

"You know leaving the academy will get you an automatic expulsion."

"I know."

He eyed me for a long moment, rubbed at his nose, and then shrugged. "Fine, I'll tell you. But when you get expelled, I want your boots." He gestured to my feet. "They are rad." He reached into his jacket pocket and pulled out a small, dark purple glass vial. He handed it to me. "You'll need this."

After I got the directions from Dionysus, I wanted to stop at my dorm room to get my jacket and my backpack. Jasmine and Georgina ambushed us the moment we walked into the room. It was obvious they had been waiting.

"What's going on?" Jasmine asked. "Someone told us you were running out of the school." She eyed Lucian, as if he'd driven me to do something crazy.

I grabbed my bag and packed it with my stuff. "I'm leaving."

"What? Why?" Georgina grabbed my bag, so I couldn't pack anymore.

"There's something I need to do."

"You'll be expelled."

"I'm willing to face that." I yanked the bag back from her.

"Is it about the earthquakes?" Jasmine asked.

I didn't know how she knew, but obviously the rumors had been flying around. I nodded.

"Then I'm coming with you."

"No you're not. You're not risking your—"

"My family lives in New Athens. If they're…" She swallowed, not wanting to voice what we were all thinking since we heard the news. "I need to know."

"Give me your address. I'll find out for you. There's no reason for you to risk everything, too."

Georgina snatched the bag from me again. "If you want to truly sneak out, you can't take your bag with you. You have to go light and quick. And you can't go now while everyone is awake. You have to leave in the middle of the night. That way you'll have at least six hours before you're missed in class."

"Georgina's right." Lucian nodded. "It's too dangerous to go now."

I looked around at everyone then my eyes landed on Jasmine. "Fine. We'll go at midnight."

She nodded, leaving our room to return to hers. It was almost curfew, and Pandora would be doing her rounds soon.

I turned to Lucian. "You need to go."

"I'll meet you at the bottom of the stairs before the entrance to Hephaistos's foundry."

I shook my head. "You've already done enough, Lucian. I can't ask you to risk anything more."

"You don't need to ask. I'll meet you down there. I'll be your diversion if you need it." And he left before I could respond.

Sighing, I sank onto my bed. Georgina sat on hers, opposite me. "Are you sure you know what you're doing?"

"No. But I have to go. I can't stay here, not knowing what happened. Earthquakes have never occurred in or around Pecunia before. Ever."

"You think it's something unnatural?"

I shrugged. "I don't know, but if something happened to Sophia and I could've done something about it, I wouldn't be able to live with myself."

She nodded, chewing on her thumbnail. "Do you think you can go and come back without being discovered?"

"I have to try."

She climbed off her bed, dropped to the floor, and

pulled out a box from underneath. She opened it and took out a small wrapped bundle, handing it to me.

I unfolded the handkerchief to reveal a small, round, green mass, almost as big as a golf ball. The strong odor wafting from it made me wrinkle my nose. It smelled like moldy cheese. "What is it?"

"A pick-me-up. It's like drinking ten energy drinks without all the sugar. It'll give you a burst of energy and strength when you need it most."

"Did you make this?"

She nodded. "With Demeter's help. She says I have a real knack for handicraft."

"You definitely have a gift, and I thank you for this." I rolled it back into the handkerchief and stuffed it into my pants' pocket.

Georgina jumped onto my bed and hugged me so tight I couldn't breathe. "I'm scared for you."

"I'll be fine, Gina."

She pulled back and stared me in the eyes. "I had a vision during prophecy class. I realize now it was about you."

"What was it?"

"I was outside on the grounds near the maze with Jasmine and Ren and Lucian, even. A giant snake slithered out from the maze and chased us. It opened its mouth, showing razor sharp teeth that were black and dripping with poison, and tried to swallow us whole."

I ran my hand down her arm and chuckled. "I'm not going to be eaten up by a snake."

"No, Melany, I'm pretty sure the snake was you."

CHAPTER FOURTEEN

MELANY

I didn't sleep. I lay awake on my bed in the dark, not only thinking about what I needed to do to get out of the academy, but about what Georgina had said—that I was the snake that swallowed everyone up. I wasn't sure how to take that. It definitely wasn't a positive connotation. I knew visions weren't literal, but I couldn't see the positive in it at all.

At midnight, I rolled out of bed and got ready to go. I patted my pants pocket to make sure the energy ball from Georgina was there, and then checked my jacket pocket to make sure I still had the vial Dionysus gave me. My stomach churned, and nerves zipped through me. I wasn't sure I could do this. I might be leading Jasmine into the abyss. I might end up dooming both of us.

Georgina whispered to me in the dark, "Good luck. Don't die out there."

"I'll try not to."

I peeked out the door into the dark corridor. It was empty. Pandora normally did her rounds at ten, which was curfew, and two in the morning. So I had a two-hour leeway to get down to the foundry and find a way out through the forge. I hoped Hephaistos wasn't in his workshop. This whole mission might be for nothing.

Sticking close to the wall and the shadows wavering there, I crept down the hallway and out onto the landing before the stone staircase to wait for Jasmine. A couple minutes later, she ran out to join me. I grabbed her hand and squeezed it, and then we carefully crept down the stairs to the main foyer.

All was quiet. There was no one around, and I didn't hear anything out of the ordinary because of the ticking of the huge clock hanging over the main doors. On silent feet, we snuck around the corner and to the stairs leading down four levels to Hephaistos's forge.

It was pitch black down the stairs. There wasn't a trace of light. If we didn't have some kind of light, we'd definitely trip down the stairs and break something. I hadn't thought to bring a flashlight, since I didn't know where I would find one. This couldn't be what stopped us.

I looked down at my hands and considered them for a moment. Then I slapped them together, very aware of the sound it made, but it had to be done, and rubbed the palms together.

Jasmine gave me a wide-eyed look and mouthed, "What are you doing?"

But it soon became evident when a soft yellow glow blossomed between my hands. Slowly, I pulled them apart to create a small ball of fire. It was enough to guide our way.

Smiling, Jasmine gave me a thumbs up. We made our way down the stairs, each step illuminated by my homemade lantern I carried in my hand. At the bottom, we waited for a minute. Lucian said he'd be here, but I didn't want him to get into any trouble. He'd directed me to Dionysus; that had been enough.

I counted to three under my breath then tapped Jasmine's arm, indicating for us to continue on. We moved two steps before I saw a very faint glow coming from the stairs. Lucian joined us at the bottom, but he wasn't alone.

"What are you doing here?" I whispered, angry.

Ren made a face. "I'm coming with you. I have family in New Athens."

I shook my head. "No. I'm not going to be responsible for all of you getting expelled."

"You're not responsible," he said. "I'm perfectly capable of making a decision on my own. And I'm coming, whether it's with you or on my own. I'd prefer to go with you, though, because I'm pretty sure you know what you're doing."

Jasmine nodded in solidarity. "I'm with Ren."

I wanted to tell them I really had no idea what I was doing. Although Dionysus had given me directions,

I didn't know what to do if they went astray. We could all end up trapped in the tunnels forever, for all I knew.

"Fine. Let's go."

We snuck up to the entrance to the foundry and peered inside. The eerie orange glow of the molten metal flowing through the narrow gutters throughout the room cast the only light. My gaze swept the area, searching for any movement. As far as I could tell, we were alone.

I looked at the dragon forge. It was a straight shot across one of the stone bridges and up a few rock steps onto the highest platform. "We need to go to the dragon forge. Follow me."

I hurried into the room, everyone following behind me. We made it across the bridge and were about to mount the steps to the platform when a clanging noise reverberated through the chamber. A voice trailed behind the metal clash; it was Hephaistos muttering to himself.

Jasmine stared at me. I stared back. She pointed to a rock jutting out of the floor where we could hide. She bolted behind it, followed by Ren, Lucian, then me. I peeked around the stone; if Hephaistos took the bridge, we would be spotted in a matter of seconds. Lucian must've realized the same thing because he grabbed my face, kissed me hard, then jumped out from behind the rock and ran down the bridge toward the fire God. My lips tingled from the kiss, and I ran my fingers over my mouth.

I went to follow him, but Jasmine grabbed my arm

and jerked me back. She shook her head. I knew she was right. Lucian had provided us with a distraction that we couldn't squander.

"What are you doing here, boy?" Hephaistos's voice boomed.

"I have a question about blast cleaning and whether we're going to do that with our shields."

"It's midnight. Why are you asking me this now?"

I peered around the rock again to see Lucian guiding Hephaistos away from the bridge, getting his back turned to us. I gestured to the others to follow me on three. I put up my fingers… one, two three…

We dashed out from the rock, up the steps in two strides, and ran to the dragon forge. The heat from it seared my face. I suspected some of my eyelashes had burned away already. The acrid odor of burning hair filled my nose.

We didn't have much time. A few minutes at most. Taking in a deep breath, I put my hands out over the fire, having faith they wouldn't burn to a crisp. Fire and I had a deep understanding. I concentrated on lowering the flames. Slowly, the fire started to recede until there were only hot red glowing coals. Grabbing an iron rod hanging from the side of the forge, I pushed the coals to the side to give us a clear path. We were going to have to crawl into the dragon's mouth. It was the only way.

I set the rod aside and clambered up into the iron forge. The heat was nearly unbearable, but I braced against it, and inched my way deep into the channel. I glanced over my shoulder to make sure Jasmine and Ren were behind me. They were, both their faces masks of discomfort. Ren looked pained, and I wondered if it was because he had an affinity to water and the heat and fire were contradicting that.

I kept moving, praying that Dionysus had given me good information. Another few feet and I saw an opening into the surrounding rock. That had to be the entrance to the tunnel. I crawled through the opening, and relief surged over me. It was a tunnel, tall enough that we could stand. For a few minutes, I'd feared we'd be crawling through the rock.

"Now what?" Jasmine asked.

"We walk through the tunnel, and then we should come to a V. We're supposed to go to the right."

"I hope Dionysus wasn't drunk when he gave you these directions."

I made a face. "Of course not." But he was. Disgustingly so. By the time he'd finished giving me instructions, he could barely stand up. Lucian and I had to help him back to his room. He sang some bawdy bar song the entire time.

We jogged through the tunnel; time was our enemy. We needed to get there and return in less than six hours. When we reached the V, we went to the right. The tunnel got narrower as we went. I wasn't claustrophobic, but my heart still picked up a few beats. After another fifteen minutes, I noticed my shoes sloshing in water, and I wondered if we were under the ocean. The thought made my heart race a bit faster.

Another fifty feet and the water rose to our ankles. Another fifty and it was to our knees.

"I don't like this, Mel." A tremor ran through Jasmine's voice.

"We'll be okay. We got Ren with us. He can make the water go away." I glanced over my shoulder at him. "Right?"

His eyes were wide, and he didn't look confident when he said, "Right."

Finally, the tunnel widened, and as we came out into a cave, the water receded. Now according to Dionysus, we had to climb some rocks to get to a door. To the right was a steep incline. I pointed to it.

"There. We have to climb."

I started up the slope thinking it was going to be easy, but it wasn't. There were a lot of loose rocks, and I slipped a few times. Jasmine almost slid all the way back down, but Ren grabbed her arm and hauled her back up. I scrambled the rest of the way up, relieved to see a small wooden door in the rock wall.

I turned the knob and opened the door. We all had to crouch down to go through it. Then we were inside a fairly narrow wooden structure. Tilting my head up, I saw there wasn't a ceiling, just a column of wood that went up one hundred feet. I reached out and touched the sides; they were rough against my fingers.

"We're in a tree."

"Are you sure?" Jasmine looked around.

Then the surface in front of us moved. A diminutive form emerged from the wood, its skin as rough and dark as tree bark, eyes the color of leaves. Tiny branches protruded from its head, almost like a set of deer antlers. It was a Dryad.

It blinked angrily at us and then spoke, its voice as crackly as dried leaves. "Who are you, and what do you want?"

"I'm Melany, this is Jasmine and Ren. We're from the academy. We need to get to New Athens and Pecunia."

"No."

I frowned. "What do you mean, no? We've come a long way to get here."

"No. Go back. I won't let you pass. It's too dangerous."

Frustrated, I smacked my hands down on my jacket. Something hard jabbed into my palm. I reached into my pocket and pulled out the small glass vial. I held it up toward the Dryad.

"This is from Dionysus."

It plucked the bottle from my fingers, its eyes wide and hungry. "Ah, bless Dionysus. You may pass. But be careful, malevolent forces are at work." It stepped to one side to reveal another door.

I pushed it open and crawled out of the tree on my hands and knees into what was once a park. When I stood, I could see, even in the dark, the destruction the earthquake had caused. The grand oak was the only tree left standing whole and untouched. The rest had either been completely pushed out of the ground, roots splayed in every direction, or broken in half, branches lying haphazardly all over the place.

"Oh, my Gods." Jasmine swung around, taking in all the damage.

"Do either of you know where we are? I don't recognize it." I gazed toward the street running along the park to see if there was a street sign anywhere.

"I'm pretty sure it's Pan Park." Ren pointed to the left. "If we go that way, we'll run into Hegemone Lane, which will take us into the center of New Athens."

"Yes, I see it now." Jasmine moved that way, and Ren and I followed.

As we made our way through town, destruction surrounded us. It looked like a war zone. Buildings and houses were in shambles. Power lines hung from poles. Nothing sparked though, as the whole town had been shut down. There was no electricity. And as we moved quickly through the empty streets, we realized we were alone.

When we reached a gated neighborhood, the placard still stood, called Vista Heights, and Ren took off at a run. Jasmine and I ran after him. He stopped in front of a two-story house, or what should've been a two-story' there was only one level left. It was really dark and hard to see anything.

Jasmine found a discarded flashlight, but the batteries were dead. She held it tight, and I could tell she was doing something to it. A few minutes later, the light flashed on. She went up to Ren's side and held it up for him. He aimed the beam at the front door.

Painted in red on the wooden door was a giant X. In the right quadrant, EVAC 5 was painted.

Ren let out a long breath of air. "They got out."

Jasmine put her arm around him, and they leaned into each other.

I was happy for Ren, but we needed to keep going. We only have maybe five hours, and Pecunia was at least an hour away. "Jasmine, how far to your house?"

She shook her head. "Not sure. By car Vista Heights would've been maybe fifteen minutes from me. Walking? It will take over an hour."

"Okay, let's get going then."

As we headed out of the neighborhood, we came across a car that still looked in shape. It had a few dings, but all the tires were good. I checked inside and saw the key was still in the ignition. We piled in and I wrapped my hands around the steering wheel holding my breath that it started. It whirred a few times, my knuckles turning white from the tight grip I had, but then it kicked over. My sigh of relief was instant. I checked the gas gauge; it was near empty, but at least it would get us closer to Jasmine's.

Twenty minutes later, I pulled the car to a stop in front of a condominium complex that was partially intact. Jasmine sprang out of the car and ran around to the back of the building. The damage in the back was worse. Half of some of the condos were completely in rubble.

Jasmine dropped to her knees, her face in her hands. I could hear her sobs. I crouched beside her and wrapped my arms around her, my heart aching for her. "Don't give up, Jas. I bet your family got out. I saw red X's on a couple of the doors at the front."

"Jasmine?"

We looked up to see an elderly black woman with grey curls picking her way over the debris on the ground. Jasmine jumped to her feet and approached her.

"Lolly?" Jasmine hugged the woman. "What are you doing here?"

"I could ask you the same thing. I thought you were at some fancy school."

"I was. I am. But when I heard about the earth-quake, I—"

Lolly rubbed Jasmine's back. "Your momma and daddy got out. Don't you worry about that."

Jasmine sagged in the older woman's arms, and my heart ached for her.

"What are you still doing here?"

"I'm on my way out. There's a van just up the street taking the last of us. I wasn't leaving without my Denzel."

I could see now the small dog squirming in her arms.

"What happened?" I asked her.

She looked over at me. Her face was haunted. "Still not too sure. I was in bed, when the whole building just shook. I got out, turned on the TV, and saw in some areas that the ground just cracked open. It almost looked like something big pushed out of the earth itself.

It was the craziest thing I'd ever seen." She shook her head. "Then the building shook again. I guess it was aftershocks, at least that's what they said on the news. Then we were told to evacuate the building. I got out of my apartment just in time before it all came crashing down."

Jasmine hugged her again, little Denzel yapping from between them. "I'm glad you're safe."

"The van's just up the street. They'll take us all out of here."

Jasmine shook her head. "We can't come with you. We have to go to Pecunia then back to the academy. No one can know we were here, Lolly."

She patted Jasmine's face. "All right. I won't say I saw you, but I may just whisper in your momma's ear that you're okay."

We wished Lolly well, and then we got back in the car and drove out of the neighborhood and on to Pecunia. It was almost an hour drive between towns, and I wasn't sure we were going to make it ten miles with an empty gas tank. My gut clenched with worry.

I was right; soon, the car puttered then rolled to a stop on the side of the dark, empty highway. I slammed my fist against the steering wheel. "Shit."

"I guess we're walking." Ren got out of the back of the car.

I stayed put as despair took its hold on me. We weren't going to make it. There was no way we could get to Pecunia and then back to a portal in three hours. I questioned if I wanted to bother going back.

They couldn't expel me if I wasn't there, could they? I mean, what would be the worst thing that could happen?

But I wanted to go back. I wanted to complete my training and become a demigod. I wanted to see Georgina. And I desperately wanted to see Lucian again. I rubbed my fingers over my lips, thinking about when he'd kissed me.

Frustrated, I leaned against the steering wheel. There had to be a way to get to Pecunia faster. As I leaned forward, the scent of old cheese wafted to my nose. The super energy ball in my pocket.

I reached in and pulled out the bundle. Georgina said it was like drinking ten Red Bulls. It was a pick-me-up. It had to be a worth a try. I unwrapped it and pinched it into three globs. I handed one to Jasmine.

She wrinkled her nose. "What is it?"

"Georgina made it. Supposed to give us a lot of energy and strength. Maybe we can run to Pecunia."

"Too bad we haven't had flying class yet. We could've flown there." She opened her mouth and plopped the wad of green dough inside. "Here goes nothing."

I got out of the car and walked over to Ren and gave him his piece. He put it in his mouth and chewed. He grimaced. "It's really gross."

I ate the last piece. It was gross. Tasted like dirt mixed with some dried grass. It was also gritty, as if it actually had some tiny bits of gravel in it. But almost instantaneously after swallowing it, I felt something inside my body. Spreading out from my stomach was a soothing heat. It soaked into every single muscle.

Ren grinned at me. "I feel pretty good."

Jasmine got out of the car. "Do you guys feel like you could bench press an elephant right about now?"

I nodded. I moved my legs up and down; they felt really strong. Energized. "I think we could run to Pecunia."

And we did. What would've taken us forty minutes to drive and hours to walk, we made it to my town in twenty-five minutes. Every muscle in my body tingled when we came to a stop in my neighborhood. It was amazing what Georgina had concocted. A superpower pellet.

As we approached the Demos estate, my guts churned. The front cast iron gate was still standing, but it hung open, holding on by one fastener. The beautiful trees lining the driveway were all broken and lying on their sides. I had faith the house would be somewhat intact. It was solidly built. But when we crested the hill, I saw I was wrong.

It was in shambles. Not one wall stood erect. It looked like a giant had taken his fist and smashed it. My heart leapt into my throat as I crossed the grounds toward the cottage. *I'm sure she got out with the rest of the family.* That thought spun around and around in my head like a carousel.

I was so anxious to get there I almost started to run, but I froze when I heard voices coming from the garden. I also heard the squawk of a police radio.

Ren and Jasmine came up beside me, and we all crept over to the hedge that was still in one piece, so we could see what was going on. There were three men dressed in black, and they had flashlights sweeping over the area. They were looking for survivors.

One of them walked over to the pile of stone and wood that would've been the cottage, casting his light over the debris. Then his light stilled as did my heart.

"I've found someone. I've found a body."

CHAPTER FIFTEEN

MELANY

*M*y knees buckled, and I would've fallen if Jasmine and Ren hadn't grabbed onto my arms and held me upright. Before I could form a coherent thought, a loud moan erupted from my throat.

"Noooo!"

Several flashlights swung toward the hedge we hid behind.

"Who's there?" one of the officers demanded as he walked toward us.

"We need to go." Jasmine pulled on my arm, but my legs weren't working. I wanted to beg her to just drop me and leave me here. She wasn't going to do that. Instead, she grabbed my hand and yanked me with her as she and Ren ran for the road.

The officers were in pursuit.

"Grab them!"

With a renewed energy, I made my legs obey me. We sprinted toward the main gate and the road.

Misjudging the debris on the ground, I tripped over a piece of one of the stone statues and fell hard to my knees. Scrambling up, I spied something shiny near my hand. I reached for it. It was a piece of a rope, a golden rope. I shoved it into my pocket as I clambered to my feet and continued to run.

Georgina's energy ball still lingered in my system, and I felt it powering up my muscles. I assumed it was the same for Jasmine and Ren, as it didn't take all of us long to dash through the iron gate and sprint down the road, the officers struggling behind us. They wouldn't be able to catch up on foot.

After we'd run for twenty minutes, we stopped and took a breather near the destroyed strip mall I'd seen on the news report.

"Are you okay?" Jasmine put her hand on my shoulder.

I didn't know how to answer that. I wasn't okay, but I knew they both needed me to be if we were going to make it back to the academy. For now, while I didn't have time to process what had happened, I nodded. When I was alone, I knew I was going to fall apart.

Ren kept watch on the road. "Do you think they'll follow us?"

We got our answer when two armored cars came roaring down the road with a huge floodlight sweeping the area. We ducked into one of the shops that still had one wall standing.

"Damn it. What are we going to do? They're blocking the road to New Athens."

I gestured to another road, the one leading out of Pecunia. "We could go to Cala. It's closer. Maybe the portal's still open."

"Why would it be?" Jasmine asked.

"I don't know, but we have to do something."

Ren's brow furrowed, as if he were deep in thought. "If it's not open, I might be able to create one. Poseidon's been teaching me."

We all agreed that was the best course of action, considering we didn't have many options and were running out of time. Although I was past believing we were going to get back to the academy undetected.

While the two vehicles drove slowly around, we kept to the dark shadows and were able to get out of the area and onto the road. Once on the open highway, we ran as fast as we could, still powered by Georgina's superpower concoction. She'd make mad money if she ever decided to mass produce and sell it in the health food industry.

We made it to Cala as the sun stained the horizon pink. Dawn was fast approaching, and we didn't have much time. The first thing I noticed as we made our way to the pier was the town had been seemingly untouched by the earthquake. They still had electricity and all the houses and buildings were undamaged. Considering that Cala was only one hundred miles away from Pecunia and New Athens, it didn't seem possible they wouldn't feel the effects in some way.

The dock was eerily quiet when we arrived, not even the waves from the ocean seemed to be making noise. In fact when I stood at the end of pier nine and looked out over the water, it seemed unnaturally calm.

"Are we ready for this?" Ren asked.

"At this point, I don't think we have a choice."

Ren dove in first, Jasmine and I followed. The water was as cold as I remembered it from the night of the invitation—maybe even colder as it was the end of November. This time we didn't have a light in the water to guide us, so we were basically swimming blind. I hoped Ren knew approximately where he was going because I didn't have any sense of direction. We could be swimming in a circle for all I knew.

Eventually, Ren stopped swimming and just floated. Jasmine and I floated up next to him. It was obvious now the portal wasn't open for us, and Ren was going to need to try and create one. Even in the dark, I could see Jasmine start to panic. I reached over and grasped her hand to try and calm her down.

Ren moved his hands around in the water. It looked like he was conducting an orchestra. After a few minutes, a soft blue glow formed in front of him. It was working. He was doing it. But then the glow collapsed in on itself and vanished. Frustration marked Ren's face as he swirled his hands around again, in sharper, more precise movements.

Jasmine tugged on my hand. I turned to see her

struggling in the water. I pulled her to me, put my mouth on hers, and blew oxygen into her. I drew back, and she gave me a thumbs up that she was okay now. I wanted to tell Ren to hurry because I knew it wouldn't last. My lungs were even starting to burn.

The blue light flared to life again, growing. A narrow whirlpool formed under the glow. Ren smiled as his creation came to be, but then his brow furrowed as his gaze darted everywhere, and his hands stopped moving. Something was wrong.

Suddenly, the whirlpool expanded until it had encompassed all three of us. Then we were violently thrust sideways through the water. The force of it sent all three of us spinning. We were being sucked through a portal, but I didn't think it was one that Ren had made.

After a few minutes of being catapulted through the portal, we came shooting up out of the water to land on the cold, hard rock of the cave. I knocked my head when I landed, making everything fade a little behind my eyes, then go sharp again. I rolled onto my back and blinked up into a few angry faces looming over me.

One of those faces belonged to Zeus. "Bring them to the auditorium. We will assemble the school for a tribunal."

Ares loomed over me and then yanked me to my feet by the back of my jacket.

The three of us were marched into the school like criminals. I was surprised someone didn't put shackles on our wrists and ankles. Jasmine shook so hard her teeth chattered. I reached over and grabbed her hand but was pulled away again. Ares looked positively gleeful with his role as jailer.

We didn't enter the academy through the front doors but around back to another entrance. Then we were led through several corridors I didn't recognize and through a set of wide double doors and into a spacious domed auditorium with 360 degree seating. It reminded me of an ancient coliseum where gladiators fought to the death for the amusement of the masses. And like those doomed gladiators, we were marched into the middle and left to stand there out in the open to await our fate.

"I'm scared."

This time I went and hugged Jasmine. "It's going to be okay."

"How?"

"I don't know, but I refuse to accept that this is the end."

Ren clenched his jaw, fighting back his fear. "I don't want to be expelled."

"Neither do I, but we all knew this could happen."

"How did they know?" Jasmine wiped at the tears welling in her eyes. "Someone told them. Do you think it was Lucian?"

I shook my head. "No. I refuse to believe that."

"It could've been, Mel," Ren said. "No one else knew."

Another set of doors opened, and all the Gods entered, lining up on the edge of the platform in a circle around us. Then through those same doors, our peers streamed into the stadium and sat in the raised rows.

I looked for Georgina and found her in the second row. Our gazes met, and she gave me a soft smile. She was probably beating herself up for letting me go on this ill-fated excursion. I wanted to tell her that it wasn't her fault. I would've gone no matter what she said or did. I was stubborn that way. She had to have known that by now.

My gaze then found Lucian. He sat not far from Georgina. His face was a mask of sadness and frustration, and it nearly broke my heart to see it. Someone had ratted us out, but I knew deep in my heart that it wasn't Lucian.

Zeus stepped forward into the center of the auditorium. "The three of you are charged with abandonment of your post. The punishment for such a crime is memory wipe and expulsion from the academy."

There was a collective gasp throughout the stadium. But I spotted one happy audience member. Revana couldn't stop smiling.

I stepped forward. "May I speak in our defense?"

"It's not a trial but go ahead." Zeus waved his hand toward me.

"The fault lies entirely with me. I convinced both Jasmine and Ren to come with me by telling them about the earthquakes in their hometowns. They wouldn't have ever known if it wasn't for me."

Jasmine bolted forward. "That's not true."

"Melany never forced us." Ren shook his head.

"I should be expelled, not them. They are great soldiers. I've been nothing but a problem. You can ask any of the professors."

Ares nodded, as did Aphrodite.

"Not true!" Jasmine came up to my side. "Melany is the best of all of us. She can—"

Zeus put up his hand to stop us from talking. "I appreciate the strength you have to fight for your friends. You have won them a second chance."

Ren put his hands over his face and shook his head.

Jasmine was about to say something that I knew she shouldn't; I grabbed her hand and squeezed it. "It's okay."

"Nothing is okay, Mel. Nothing."

Zeus nodded to Ares, and he came over to me and Jasmine. He took her arm. "Let's go." He nodded to Ren.

Before she was led away, Jasmine wrapped her arms around me. "I'll never forget you. Ever."

I swallowed, not wanting to shed tears in front of everyone. No, I would shed my tears when I was alone. Which was going to be soon. I could handle the expulsion and never going back to Pecunia, but not being able to remember my friends or Lucian was a dagger to the heart. It was cruel and inhumane. I would do anything not to have that happen. I would suffer through any other punishment.

Ares led my friends off the platform and back into the crowd of recruits. Jasmine and Ren both took up seats by Georgina, who reached out and grabbed their hands. Solidarity. They were going to need it. I hoped they stuck together no matter what. They made a great team.

Once Ares returned to the circle of Gods, Zeus raised his hands, ready to pass my sentence. But I had one more thing to say before he condemned me.

"Those weren't earthquakes that destroyed Pecunia and New Athens."

A murmur rushed through the stadium. A few of the Gods glanced at each other.

"I saw the cracks in the ground. It looked like something pushed out of the earth. The damage was secluded to just those two towns and nowhere else. That's not how earthquakes behave."

I thought for sure Zeus was going to shut me up, but he actually looked interested in what I had to say. I reached into my pocket and pulled out the piece of golden rope. "I found this at my childhood home among the devastation." I held it up for everyone to see. There were some surprised whispers in the crowd. "It's not an ordinary piece of rope. It looks like something enchanted. Something magical. Something one of the Gods would possess."

That started a major stir.

Aphrodite stepped forward. "She's lying. She'll say anything to get out of her punishment."

"Why are we listening to this?" Ares bellowed. "She broke the rules. There isn't any room for discussion."

I noticed Hera, Apollo, and Athena nod in agreement. Demeter, Hephaistos, and Dionysus remained tight-lipped, which I appreciated. The other Gods looked beyond bored. Like they had a million other things to do today besides destroying my life and sending me into exile.

Zeus approached me and took the rope. He ran his fingers over it, frowning. "You found this in the earth-quake zone?"

I nodded.

"It doesn't change anything, Zeus." Aphrodite approached him.

He met her gaze and it wasn't friendly. "I will decide whether it changes anything or not."

She returned to her spot in the circle with a pout.

"Melany Richmond, you have proven to be resourceful, resilient, and fearless. Three traits I admire, especially in a soldier. You have moved me to give you an opportunity to stay in the academy."

There was some clapping and cheers from my peers.

"You can't be serious?" Ares blurted.

Relief surged over me. I couldn't believe I'd convinced the almighty Zeus to give me a second chance. I met my friends' gazes and smiled.

"I will give you a choice." Zeus turned to the crowd as if to regale them. "Accept a bolt of my lightning, or be expelled and thrown into exile."

"No. She'll be killed!" Demeter bolted forward.

All the blood left my head, and I thought I was going to pass out.

I looked out at the crowd and saw Lucian on his feet. "Don't do it, Blue."

"No," Jasmine and Georgina both shouted. "Mel. It's not worth your life!"

I looked at my friends and Lucian. I never wanted to forget them. The thought of it churned my stomach. What would I be without my memories of them, of this place? I'd be empty and alone for the rest of my life. What kind of life would that be? Not one worth living, that was for sure.

Swallowing down any fear I had, I lifted my head proudly. "I'll do it."

CHAPTER SIXTEEN

LUCIAN

I couldn't sit and watch this. It was wrong. I tried to dash out into the stadium—I wasn't sure what I was going to do, but I had to do something—but Heracles, who had been sitting in the rows with the students, grabbed me before I could.

"You can't stop it, Lucian."

"The lightning will kill her. She's not ready to control it."

"She's strong. Stronger than you think."

Zeus held his arms up toward the murmuring crowd, and a crack of thunder zipped in the air over head. "Silence."

That stopped everyone from talking.

"Everyone needs to witness the bravery of this girl, as she attempts the lightning trial."

Melany walked to the middle of the arena and stood there waiting. She looked so courageous out there on her own, preparing to undergo the most dangerous and most difficult trial of the academy training. I wanted to go to her, hold her hand, hug her, and tell her how I truly felt for her before it was too late.

"During the trial, Melany will have to hold my greatest and most powerful weapon crafted for me by the great cyclops, Arges—the lightning bolt."

Zeus clapped his hands together causing a loud crash of thunder to reverberate through the stadium, making everyone jump. The floor shook from the power of it. Then he slowly drew his hands apart. In between them the air sparked and crackled, until he'd formed a five-foot long bolt of glowing white lightning.

I could feel the power of it, even from where I stood. The little hairs on my arms lifted, and I could taste ozone on my tongue.

Zeus stepped toward Melany, whose face paled with every step he took.

"She will need to pick it up and hold it for no less than two minutes. There have only been ten recruits in the past one hundred years able to complete this trial. And they have gone on to glory as part of my clan."

Rearing his hand back, Zeus stuck the lightning bolt into the floor in front of Melany. She jumped back in surprise. Zeus moved back and waved his hand toward her. "You may start."

A tense hush fell over the arena. I couldn't sit and

watch, so I stood beside Heracles just on the edge of the main platform. I dug my fingernails into the palms of my hands to keep me grounded. Nerves rooted deep in my gut, and I felt nauseated as Melany took a step forward.

She closed her eyes for a moment, lifted her head, and I saw her lips move. Was she praying? I could've told her it was useless, as all the Gods were standing in this room, most of them indifferent to what was going on. No one was going to rescue her.

When she opened her eyes again, she took a wide stance, then wrapped her hands around the bolt, and picked it up. Her face instantly contorted in pain as the electricity shot through her. There were several shocked gasps in the audience. I looked over to see Georgina and Jasmine clutching hands, their eyes wide in horror as they watched their friend be tortured.

Seconds ticked by and Melany still held the lightning. Her whole body shook with the effort. Even from here, I could see her hands had turned red, burned from the heat of the electrical current pulsing through the bolt. I couldn't believe she still held it. By the looks on the Gods' faces, they couldn't believe it, either. Zeus looked practically gleeful.

After a minute, the glow of the lightning intensified, and sparks started to flare, and I wondered if Zeus had done that on purpose. But his face told me that what was happening wasn't anticipated. Frowning, he moved toward Melany. Was he going to put a stop to it?

Just as he went to reach for the bolt, zigzags of white lightning surged up Melany's arms. She opened her mouth and let out a blood-curdling scream as more waves wrapped around her body from head to toe until she was entombed in crackling white bolts.

People in the stands jumped to their feet.

"Stop it!"

"It's killing her!"

I tried to push past Heracles, but he held me firm. I watched in horror as Melany was consumed by the lightning. But then I saw something dark swirling around her; it was like black smoke curling up from the floor. It weaved in with the electrical current, surrounding her body.

Demeter broke ranks and ran toward the spectacle. "Put a stop to this. Now. You've proven your power."

Even Hephaistos and Dionysus rushed forward.

Zeus reached over and grasped the bolt in one hand and yanked it out of Melany's grip. The second that happened, she dropped to the floor like a puppet without strings.

Apollo moved out of the circle and crouched beside Melany. I could see him checking her pulse on her neck and then picking up her wrist.

I pressed against Heracles again. "Let me go." If Apollo said she was dead, I was going to hurt someone. I was going to make someone pay.

He nodded to Zeus. "She's alive."

"She did it," someone from the crowd yelled. "She held it for over two minutes."

There were a few cheers and some clapping, but for the most part, everyone was a bit stunned at what we'd just witnessed. I wasn't sure what to call it. It was supposedly a trial, but it felt like corporal punishment. Torture even.

Heracles smacked me on the back, but not as hard as he usually did it. "You see? She's strong."

"She could've died, Heracles."

His smile faded, and he bent toward my ear. "It was a message. You and your friends would do well by heeding it." He moved away from me.

"Take her to the infirmary," Zeus said, his voice no longer commanding.

Chiron pushed through the crowd that had started to gather around the platform, everyone craning their necks to get a glimpse of Melany on the floor. Once people saw him, they made room. Standing close to seven feet tall, the centaur was very imposing. Apollo gathered Melany in his arms and very gently draped her over Chiron's back, and then together they left the stadium.

"Classes are canceled today," Zeus said. "Everyone return to your dorms."

It was a bit of chaos as recruits and Gods and others streamed out of the auditorium. I caught up with Georgina, Jasmine, and Ren as they exited through the main doors.

"Do you think they'll let us see her?" Georgina asked.

Jasmine shook her head. She looked worn out. "I doubt it."

"I can't believe that just happened." Ren rubbed at his mouth, and then his voice went low. "It was almost like they wanted to kill her."

I looked at each of them, wondering if I should tell them what Heracles had said to me. "I think we need to be careful from now on and don't trust anyone. Especially not any of the professors."

"Who do you think ratted us out?" Jasmine's gaze was pointed, and I assumed she suspected me.

"I don't know, but I'm definitely going to find out."

She nodded to me, and I hoped that meant she believed me. Because if she thought I had informed on them, then maybe Melany did, too, and I couldn't live with that. Especially not after what she'd just gone through.

"Jasmine!"

The voice came from behind us. Jasmine turned just as Mia shoved through a few people and launched herself at the other girl. She wrapped her arms around Jasmine and hugged her tight.

"I was so scared. I thought you were——"

"I'm fine, Mia." She gave Mia a soft smile.

We walked together through the corridor, and when we rounded the corner to head to the main foyer and the staircase to the dorms, Dionysus was there, leaning up against the wall.

"Lucian, mate, we need to have a little chit chat."

Ren gave me a look of concern, but I shrugged it off. "You guys go ahead. I'll catch up to you later."

"Let's go to my office."

I followed Dionysus down another hall, up some stairs, then down another empty corridor until he stopped in front of a very ornate wooden door. All the carvings were versions of him dancing, or singing, or engaging in some suggestive activities with what looked like wood nymphs. He opened the door and we went in.

His office was dark and cramped with all manner of things: velvet covered chairs, round wooden tables stacked with glass jars and small boxes, piles of books and scrolls, shelves crammed with bottles of different colored liquids, and herbs and other plant based things that smelled horrible. He gestured for me to sit in one of the chairs, and he sat behind a very heavy-looking mahogany desk. He leaned back in his chair and put his feet up on the desk. There was a hookah on the desk, and he took a puff. He offered it to me, but I shook my head.

"So, that was sure something."

"I didn't tell anyone about you, if that's what you're wondering."

He pointed at me. "That is what I was wondering. I'd hate to be tortured like your friend Melany." He made a face. "She did do well, though. Surprised the crap out of Zeus I'm sure."

"Someone did talk, though."

His eyes narrowed. "And you're wondering whether

I did?" He drew his feet off the desk and leaned in toward me. "I can assure you, mate, that would be the last thing I would do. Do you honestly think we're not all ruled with the same iron fist? Zeus likes his power and likes to wield it on whomever he wants."

I sagged in the chair. Everything was starting to weigh on me, especially what had happened to Melany. I couldn't get the image of her suffering out of my mind. Her scream still echoed in my head. I knew it would haunt my dreams for a very long time.

"Look, I'm really sorry for what happened to your girlfriend. It was a terrible thing to watch. But she'll heal. Chiron is a fantastic medic. And with my potions, she'll be up and about in no time."

"I want to see her."

He put a hand to his chest. "I'm not sure how I can help you there."

I gave him a look. "How do I get into the infirmary?"

"You can go now, mate." He waved a hand toward the door.

"I'm not leaving until you tell me how I can see Melany."

He opened his mouth and made a sighing noise. "You're going to be the death of me."

"You're immortal. You can't die."

He waved a hand at me. "It's a figure of speech, saying just how annoying you are." He stood and walked to one of the shelves behind the desk. When he turned back, he had a silver flask in his hand. He gave it to me. "Give this to Chiron. It'll buy you a few minutes with her I'm sure."

I tucked the flask into my pocket and left his office. Before I went by the infirmary, I snuck by the kitchen and stole a chocolate cupcake. I wrapped it up carefully and put it in my front jacket pocket. When I arrived at the infirmary, there was a lot of activity nearby, so I had to wait. Zeus, Hephaistos, Demeter, Ares, and Aphrodite all came and went, bickering amongst themselves the whole time. After the corridor emptied, I quickly walked to the main door of the infirmary. I was about to slip inside when I felt a huge presence behind me.

I whipped around and came face to chest with Chiron.

"What are you doing here? You're supposed to be in your dorm. I'll give you five minutes to get lost before I—"

I thrust the flask toward him. "Dionysus sends his regards."

His eyes narrowed as he looked at me, then the flask. At first I didn't think he was going to take it, but then he snatched it from my fingers. He uncapped it, sniffing whatever was inside. "You have ten minutes."

I stepped into the gloomy room; the only light came from a couple of lamps flickering in sconces on the walls. There were twenty small beds in two rows, one on each side of the room. They were all empty, save one. I could see Melany's blue hair spread out over the white pillow.

She was on her back, and her eyes were closed when I approached. I took in the ashen pallor of her skin and the hollowness of her cheeks and my stomach clenched. As I settled on the edge of the bed, her eyes blinked open.

"Hey, Blue."

"Hey." Her voice was hoarse and she grimaced.

I picked up the cup of water on the table beside her bed and bent the straw for her, so she could take a sip. When she sat up, the sheet fell away from her neck and shoulder, and I saw the red puckered scars branching out across her skin. It looked like spider-webbed lightning on her body. A wave of cold surged through me. I had trouble swallowing as I took the damage in.

"Oh, Blue…" I didn't have the words.

She lifted her arm to show me more of the scars that coiled from her shoulder to her wrist. "I'm told they'll be permanent." Her voice cracked a little, and she licked her lips. "I guess I'll fit right in with these Gods and monsters."

"You're not a monster." I wrapped a tendril of her hair around my finger and gave it a little playful tug. "You're still beautiful."

That made her smile.

"I'm sorry you had to go through that."

"Yeah, not how I thought my day was going to start." She snorted and then grimaced as her body shifted in the bed.

"Were you able to find out what happened to your adoptive mother?"

She swallowed, a few tears rolling down her cheeks. "She didn't make it out."

"Oh Blue, I'm so sorry."

I reached up and brushed her tears away with my thumb. I wished I could wipe away all her pain as easily. But I knew that it would be impossible.

I put my hand in my jacket pocket and took out the cupcake; it was all mushed now. I unwrapped it for her. "I know this isn't going to stop the pain, but it might help a little."

She took it from me. "Thank you. I'm starving." She took a big bite and icing stuck at the side of her mouth.

Chuckling, I wiped the chocolate icing off with my thumb, lingering a little longer than was probably wise. I licked it off my thumb, when what I wanted to do was kiss her long and hard.

We locked eyes, and for a moment everything fell away. I bent down to her mouth and was about to touch my lips to hers when someone coughed from the door.

"Time to go, Romeo."

Startled, I got to my feet and bumped her bed, jostling her a bit. She grimaced. I winced. "I'm sorry."

She chuckled. "It's fine."

"I'll see you later, okay?"

Melany grabbed my hand before I could walk away. "Thank you, Lucian. For the cupcake… and for helping me get out. It means a lot to me."

"You're welcome. Just get better. Hand-to-hand combat won't be the same without you to spar with."

I left the infirmary, feeling both joy and despair. My emotions were so mixed up about Melany I didn't know what to do. All I knew for certain was that I liked her. More than I ever thought was possible. And that was scarier than facing any of the Gods' trials.

CHAPTER SEVENTEEN

MELANY

J spent fourteen days in the infirmary before Chiron said I was fit enough to go back to my dorm and to resume my training. Fourteen days of extreme boredom and bland, unappetizing food. I was only allowed visitors for a few hours in the day, and I was thankful for the snacks my friends snuck in for me.

The first three days I spent lying in bed, unable to move much. I'd been mostly sedated during that time while Chiron tried to heal the scars networking across most of my body from the lightning. Pain had been my constant companion during those days. After that I'd been able to sit up, talk, eat, and accept visitors.

The first time Jasmine saw me with my brand new lightning scar, she cried. Georgina was a little bit more reserved, but not by much. Ren told me I looked badass. And Lucian, when he snuck in after hours, told me how beautiful I was.

I also received visits from Demeter; she brought me some books to read, and one time Hephaistos popped his head in, grunted at me, checked my hands to make sure they weren't too badly damaged and I could still work with fire, and then left just as quickly.

During the down time, I tried to get as much sleep as I could, as I was beyond exhausted, and my entire body ached. But it proved hard, especially since most times when I closed my eyes, I kept seeing the pile of rubble that used to be my cottage and hearing the voice of the police officer saying he'd found a body. Not being active gave me too much time to think. Too much time to cry.

By the time I went back to class, I was completely empty of tears.

My first class back was elemental. When I walked into the training facility, there were a lot of stares at my newly acquired, full-body network of scars and whispers behind hands. But to my surprise, there were also some high fives, even from a few people I was not expecting.

Diego approached me, a bit sheepishly, to my delight. "Hey Melany, I just want to say that what you did with that lightning was freaking hardcore."

"Thank you, Diego."

He held out his hand to me and I shook it. "And I dig your scar."

When he returned to his group at the water tank, I

caught Lucian's gaze, and I wondered if he had a little chat with his friend. He gave me a sly grin, and I returned it, with my heart fluttering a little bit extra.

"No time for making goo goo eyes, girl." I jumped back as Hephaistos poked me in the gut with the iron tongs. "It's your turn to make some fire balls; you're behind in the class."

I opened my mouth to say, "Hey, I was in the infirmary for fourteen days." But he shook his head. "I don't want to hear any of your excuses."

"Fine." I walked up to the main fire pit where the flames flickered up five feet in the air.

I lifted my hands, hesitant to spread them out toward the fire. Sometimes, they still hurt when I used them too much. Chiron had given me salve for them, and they were healing, but every now and then I got a sharp pain.

Taking in a deep breath, I opened my hands and thrust them toward the fire pit. The flames instantly danced toward me, as if they were greeting me. Saying hello, welcome back. I smiled and coaxed the flames to me, until tendrils actually wrapped around my fingers.

Jasmine and Georgina, who were nearby watching, gasped in surprise as I gathered the fire into my hands. I moved them around, caressing the flames, molding them into the shape I wanted. I kept at it until I had a sphere of fire between my palms about the size of a basketball. I looked at Hephaistos over the glowing red ball.

I saw his lips twitch up into a smile, but then he

immediately turned away and frowned at something someone else was doing. I couldn't win with him.

Pleased with the result of my firecraft, I bounced the ball in my hands, wishing I could toss it at something. Or someone. The prime target was glaring at me from across the facility. Revana was never going to be happy until I was either expelled or dead. I wanted to ask her, "Wasn't my torture enough for you?" Obviously it wasn't, as she still hate-stared at me like I'd stolen something from her.

My gaze then landed on Lucian. *Bingo. We have a winner.*

I didn't steal him, as he was a person and not a possession, but I was sure he wasn't her boyfriend. During one of his secret visits to the infirmary, I had asked him about Revana, and why he hung out with her. He'd told me because he didn't know better. But now he did. That had made me grin like a love-struck fool.

When we were switching stations to work with shadows, Lucian's group and mine passed each other. Lucian grabbed my arm and pulled me away from the group.

"I was going to mention this before, and I probably should have, but I didn't want to bring it up so soon after…"

"Go on. You got me curious now."

"When you were going through your trial and the lightning was wrapping around you, I saw… well, I think I saw a shadow protecting you. Putting some kind of barrier between you and the lightning."

I frowned. "You think Erebus protected me in some way?"

He shrugged. "I don't know. I'm just telling you what I saw." He ran his hand down my arm, then he returned to his group, and I went to mine.

Erebus materialized in front of us. Today, he wore a top hat and carried a silver-tipped, black cane to go with his gothic look.

"Welcome back, Melany." He gave a little bow.

I pressed my lips together in a facsimile of a smile. I wasn't sure if he was being sincere or patronizing. He had that arrogant air about him.

"Today, we are going to learn how to manipulate the shadows, to control them, not to just be able to camouflage inside them."

He held out his right hand, and after a few seconds, tendrils of darkness coiled around his fingers, then he circled his hand in front of him, and the black smoke made a loop in the air. Then he flicked his hand toward me, and that smoke loop wrapped around my wrist. Erebus flicked his hand backwards, and I was tugged forward by my arm. He'd lassoed me with a rope of shadow.

Everyone laughed as I stumbled forward.

Erebus closed his hand, and the shadow rope vanished, releasing me. "Get into pairs and practice. First, make the shadow rope, then try to catch your partner with it." Since we were only a mere foot apart, he turned to me. "You can be my partner, Melany, since the group is uneven."

I almost let out a disgruntled groan but kept it bottled inside. I glanced over at Jasmine and Georgina. They both gave me concerned looks and I shrugged. Nothing I could do about it.

I faced off with Erebus. He gave me a creepy smile as I lifted my hand and moved it through the permanent shadows swirling around us. Within seconds, I was able to manipulate the darkness through my fingers, making a circle in the air.

Erebus nodded. "Not bad. You take to the shadows easily, I think."

Throwing it was a whole other matter. Every time I flung my hand forward, the smoke rope dissipated, and I had to start all over again.

Under Erebus's eagle eye, I created the smoke rope again, and this time when I threw it, I was able to get it around his arm. I almost threw a fist into the air. Instead, I yanked on the rope and moved Erebus forward.

He smiled and tapped his cane on the floor; we were completely cloaked in darkness, and he was only a couple of inches away. He grabbed my arm hard.

"Who saved you?"

"What? I don't know what you're talking about."

"During the trial. I saw the shadows shroud you. Without them, you would have certainly died."

I tried to pull away from him, but his grip was solid.

His fingers dug into my flesh. "I don't know what you're talking about."

But I did. Lucian had mentioned the same thing. He had insinuated Erebus had been the one to save me, but obviously that wasn't the case. So who had?

"You're being protected, that much is obvious." His hand tightened around my arm. "But understand this, Melany Richmond, that kind of protection comes with a cost."

I managed to wrench myself out of his grip, then the shadows fell away, and we were visible again. Flustered, I looked around at the others, but they were busy engaged in lassoing each other. I didn't think they had even noticed we'd disappeared.

After class I wasn't sure if I should tell Jasmine and Georgina what had happened. I was definitely going to tell Lucian next chance we got to be alone, which wasn't going to be any time soon, as we were ushered to our next class. The art of flying, which was a special lesson of transformation training.

The training was going to take place outside, and the reason for it was immediate as Hermes flew in with large, golden wings flapping and landed on the field in front of us. As we all gaped in awe, he folded his wings behind him and walked toward us.

"Good afternoon. Welcome to flying class." Smiling, he looked at everyone. Out of all the Gods, Hermes was the most affable. He honestly didn't look much older than we were, and always wore a buttoned-up shirt tucked into khaki pants and a bowtie. His dark brown hair always looked a bit unruly, and he constantly tucked it behind his ears.

"Today, I'm going to teach you how to fly. I know this may seem like an impossible feat, but I assure you, it is possible for every single one of you. You are here at this academy for a reason. Because you all have Gods' blood running through your veins. And it's through that you will be able to fly."

Heracles joined us out on the field, and I got a little bit nervous.

"Now, learning to fly is really quite easy…" Hermes walked around then grabbed onto Diego, his wings unfurled, and they lifted into the sky.

Diego's face was comical, and I would've laughed if Hermes wasn't taking him up three hundred feet into the air. My stomach flipped over as I craned my neck and looked up at them, hovering in the sky. Nervous chatter rippled among the group.

"Vertigo ignites the fear of falling, hiding our will to fly." Hermes's voice boomed down to us. "So we must find our will to fly."

Then he dropped Diego.

Diego's screams echoed throughout the field as he fell. Before he hit the ground, Heracles was there. He caught him effortlessly and then set him onto his feet again. Diego leaned over and vomited.

Hermes fluttered back down to the ground. "Who wants to try?"

Everyone glanced nervously at each other. Then Lucian's arm shot up. "I'll go."

"Excellent."

Hermes grabbed Lucian, and they shot up into the air. My heart leapt into my throat, seeing him up so high. Then Hermes dropped him, and I put my hand over my mouth to stop the gasp.

Right before Lucian hit dirt, crimson wings popped out from his shoulder blades, and he hovered in midair. He hung there ten feet above us, looking like a God. A gorgeous, golden God who took my breath away.

Hermes flew down to hover beside him. "Well done, Lucian." He beamed at him. "Now, who wants to go next?"

Several hands shot up into the air.

One by one, each student went up into the sky with Hermes and came down with wings. It took a few people a couple of tries, but eventually everyone produced ruby-red wings, even Revana, who unfortunately looked like a stunning Goddess.

I was the last to go. I really didn't like heights.

Hermes stepped up to me. "Well, Miss Richmond, it's now or never."

Jasmine touched my shoulder. "You can do it, Mel. It's easier than it looks. Honestly."

I didn't want to disagree with her and tell her I didn't believe her one bit.

Hermes grabbed onto my arms, flying us up into the air. My stomach dropped, and for a moment I thought I might retch. But I kept it together, focusing my gaze on him and not the hard ground four hundred feet beneath us and sudden, crushing death.

"Are you ready?"

I shook my head. "No."

"Good. Then that's the perfect time to do something great."

He let me go. I plummeted to the earth.

I squeezed my eyes shut, not wanting to see the ground as it came up to meet me, and thought about flying. How cool it would be. How amazing I would be flying around. How I was made of the power of wind.

I thought it would take me mere seconds to reach the ground. But somehow I still wasn't there.

Then I heard loud gasps beneath me.

"Oh my Gods!"

"How is that possible?"

"Mel! You're breathtaking."

Slowly, I opened my eyes. I wasn't a pancake on the ground; I was floating in the air. I could feel the rush of wind coming from behind me, along my cheeks. I looked down at the faces gaping up at me, and wondered why everyone looked so stunned. Hadn't I produced wings like they had?

Hermes landed on the ground, reaching up and tugging on my foot. "Come down. Now."

Surprised by the concern in his voice, I flapped my wings once and then settled down onto the ground. He hurried behind me, touching my back.

I looked to Lucian. "What's going on?"

His smile nearly cracked his face. "Your wings, Blue. Look at your wings."

Twisting my head, I looked over my shoulder to see

huge, luxurious black wings protruding from my shoulder blades. Black, not red like everyone else's.

"Uh, what the hell is going on?" I could hear the quaver in my voice.

Hermes lightly touched my shoulder. "You stay here." He turned to the group. "Everyone else, please return to the school."

Hermes then shot up into the sky and flew toward the outer building.

I looked at Jasmine, Georgina, Ren, and Lucian, pleading with them to stay with me, but they were herded away by Heracles. I heard a few people's remarks as they moved back into the school.

"What do black wings mean?"

"Means she's defective."

I recognized that voice easily. Revana was obviously getting a kick out of this.

A few minutes later, Hermes returned with Zeus and Aphrodite, who were all flying in on golden wings.

The moment Aphrodite saw me she sucked in a breath. "How grotesque."

Zeus walked around me, poked at my back, and ran his fingers over my feathers. That was a strange sensation that pulled at my belly. It didn't feel good and made me a bit queasy. It was probably going to take a bit to be comfortable with the fact that I had wings, let alone black ones.

After some more intrusive poking and prodding, Zeus stood in front of me. "You can pull your wings in now."

I did, the feeling of them receding into my body sending a shiver over the rest of me. "Do you know why I have black wings? Is it really bad? Am I diseased or something?"

He shook his head. "No, you're not diseased."

"Then why? Did I do something wrong?"

"We need to confer with the other Gods. I suggest you return to your dorm with your peers."

I walked toward the doors to the school, but instead turned left to go out into the school grounds. I didn't want to be bombarded with a million questions that I didn't have an answer to. I needed some time alone to figure it out. There had to be a logical reason why I had black wings and everyone else had red ones. Maybe it had something to do with what I'd endured during the lightning trials. Maybe it had literally burned inside my body.

CHAPTER EIGHTEEN

MELANY

I didn't really know where I was going until I rounded the corner of the academy and spotted the tall hedge maze. No one would think to find me in there. I'd gone through the maze once before with Georgina and Jasmine; it was a bit harder on my own. I ran into three dead ends before I found my way to the center.

The moment I saw the white wooden gazebo in the middle, I heard music playing, the strains of something classical. As I got closer, I spotted a man in a dark purple suit jacket and slacks sitting inside the gazebo, strumming a guitar.

He looked up and smiled when I approached. "Hello there, Melany."

"Hey?" I'd never seen him before. I would've definitely remembered, as he was strikingly good looking with sharp cheekbones, a strong jaw with a bit of scruff, and large, dark eyes under thick, dark eyebrows. He had dark hair that was swept back off his forehead and curled around his ears.

"How's your day been?"

I sat on the bench across from him. "Not so good. Been kind of weird." I tilted my head to study him. "Who are you, exactly?"

He stopped strumming and met my gaze. "Hades. Surely, you've heard of me."

Although I didn't want him to see my surprise, I couldn't stop my eyes from widening. A little rush of adrenaline spiked through my body. Hades was a legend. The ruler of the underworld had a bit of a reputation. I was surprised to see him here, as I didn't think he was welcome at the academy by the way I'd heard some of the Gods talk about him.

"What are you doing here?" I gestured to the gazebo.

"Playing a little guitar, chilling out a bit. I like to come here when no one is around." He ran his thumb over the strings. The sound vibrated against my skin, making me shiver. "What are you doing here? Running away?"

"I'm not running away. I just needed a little time to myself to think."

"About what?"

I snorted. "You ask a lot of questions."

"I'm a curious kind of guy." He grinned.

"Well, if you must know, I kind of sprouted black wings instead of red wings during flying with Hermes."

He laughed. "Oh, I bet Hermes lost his mind, didn't he?"

I smiled. "Maybe a little."

"Then he flew off to grab old Zeus and whoever else to confer about this shocking occurrence, I'll bet."

"Yeah, he did."

Hades shook his head. "Typical. And I imagine after a lot of poking and prodding and humming and hawing, they didn't tell you a damn thing, right?"

I nodded.

"That's why they don't like me around here, and why I've never been part of the academy. Because I tell the truth. I don't hide it away from you."

"And what's the truth?"

"That you're different. And it's awesome that you are" He played a few notes. "They're scared of different. Different upsets their status quo."

I eyed him, unsure if he was feeding me a bunch of crap. Although he'd have no motive to do so. He wasn't even part of the academy. And he was right. They definitely didn't like different.

"You should embrace your differences, Melany. It's what makes you special. It's what makes you powerful."

"Blue? You in here?"

I looked up to see Lucian heading toward the gazebo. I smiled as he approached. "How did you know I was in here?"

"I may have not gone back to the dorms and hung

around waiting for you. I saw you run over to the maze."

I turned to introduce him to Hades but he was gone. I hadn't even seen him get up and leave. The only thing that indicated he'd even existed was a guitar pick lying on the stone bench he'd been sitting on.

"What are you doing out here?"

"I was just talking to Hades."

Frowning, Lucian's gaze swept the gazebo. "Hades?"

"Yeah, he was just sitting there, playing his guitar." I pointed to the bench. "We were talking about the academy and my black wings."

Lucian sat on the bench beside me. "Blue, I didn't see anyone else when I came around the corner toward the gazebo. Just you."

I grimaced. "No, he was right there." I pointed to the bench.

"I'm sorry, but it's impossible that Hades would be here. He's not allowed to step on school grounds. There are wards or something preventing him."

I got up and went over to the other bench and picked up the guitar pick. "Then how do you explain this?"

He shrugged. "Maybe it belongs to Dionysus. I've seen him around the academy carrying a guitar."

I shook my head. That couldn't be right. He'd been here. I'd talked to him. It wasn't a figment of my imagination. But maybe I shouldn't press the issue. I didn't want Lucian thinking I was any crazier then he probably already did.

"Maybe you're still tired from the trial. I can't believe you're actually walking around after that." He got to his feet and came toward me. "And today was—"

"Messed up?"

"I was going to say amazing. You have black wings. It's wicked cool."

I made a face. "It's not cool. It's weird. Zeus and the others poked at me like I was some science experiment."

He grabbed my hand. "It's not weird. You're not weird. You're… special."

Hades's words played in my head again. What was so special about me?

"I bet everyone else thinks I'm weird."

"Screw everyone else." He tugged me closer to him. I looked up into his face, enjoying the way the gold flecks in his eyes sparked. "I think your wings are sexy."

I made a face, pressing my lips together. My heart skipped a few beats. Flutters started low in my belly. "Sexy?"

"Yup." He ran his fingers over my shoulder. "I'd love to see them again."

I knew what he was doing. Making me feel better about my wings. Who knew Lucian was so damn sweet? I wouldn't have ever thought that upon our first meeting. I'd thought he was a bit of a jerk.

He pulled me out of the gazebo and into the open.

"If you show me yours, I'll show you mine." His sly grin made every muscle in my body quiver.

"What if I can't do it without being dropped?"

"Just try."

I took a few steps away because I couldn't coherently standing next to him. I squared my shoulders, concentrated on what I wanted to do, and then closed my eyes. Within seconds I could feel ripples up and down my back, then a bit of pressure, then…

My wings unfurled out of my shoulder blades and spread until they nearly touched the shrub wall. I grinned in triumph.

Lucian beamed at me. "They're commanding. Just like you."

"You think I'm commanding?"

He put up his fingers, spacing them an inch apart. "Just a bit."

Laughing, I pushed him. "Ha! You're a funny guy."

He took a step back, swirled around, and BAM! Out popped his wings. He flapped them once, and then they curled around him a little like a red shield.

I actually sighed at the sight of him. He looked more God-like then the Gods themselves. And I'm pretty sure he noticed because he grabbed my hand. "Let's go flying."

"What? I don't think we learned that part."

He shrugged, wings fluttering in the process. "How hard could it be?"

I hesitated for a moment, considering all the things I could've been doing. Sitting in my dorm room worrying about the implication of my black wings, or wondering why I saw Hades in the gazebo and Lucian didn't. And decided that being here with Lucian, about to fly together for the first time, was the most exciting moment of my life and one I shouldn't squander.

"Okay. Let's do it."

I spread my wings out as far as they could go and then flapped them once to get the hang of it. I flapped them again and again, and the power of it lifted me off the ground. Soon, I was hovering in midair over the gazebo. Lucian joined me.

Then I winked at him and was off like a shot. I could feel the power of flying surging through my body. It was euphoric. I did a quick glance over my shoulder to see Lucian easily catching up to me, a grin on his face.

I flew up as high as the spire on the main tower of the academy then zipped to the right and soared around the citadel, swooping down toward the training field, then up again. Lucian was right on my heels, never breaking form. He was gorgeous to watch, like a golden bird of prey, powerful and majestic.

He swooped in along my side, the very tips of our wings nearly touching. Together, we veered around the east wing of the school, past the dorms. If anyone had been looking out their windows, they would've seen Lucian spiral up into the air, like a blazing red and gold tornado. When he swooped down, he tapped my shoe, and then shot off toward one of the towers. *Tag. You're it.*

Laughing I caught up to him, as he landed on the upper most balcony of the academy. He folded in his wings just as I landed beside him. We leaned against the railing and looked out over the vast grounds surrounding the school. I spotted areas I didn't even know existed. There was an expansive wood over the horizon. The land looked like it went on forever.

"It's beautiful here."

"It is."

I turned my head slightly to see Lucian staring at me and not the view. My cheeks flushed at the avid attention he gave me.

"You're not even looking."

He reached up and stroked his fingers over my cheek. "Oh, believe me, I'm looking."

My belly flip-flopped and I swallowed nervously. It wasn't that I'd never been intimate with a boy before. I had back in Pecunia. But it wasn't anything like this. The boy wasn't anything like Lucian, and I never felt this kind of intensity just standing near him, with just his fingertips caressing my skin.

A shiver rushed down my body, and I trembled a little.

"Are you cold?" He took a step closer.

I shook my head.

He inched even closer, until we were just a breath apart. Slowly, he moved his fingers down and traced a line along my jaw. Then with one finger, he tilted my chin up and softly brushed his lips against mine.

I couldn't stop the tiny intake of breath, and he

kissed me again, this time sweeping his tongue lightly against mine. The intensity of it, of him, took over, and I buried my hands in his golden waves and moved my mouth over his, tasting and teasing.

We kissed on that romantic balcony until the sun went down. It was positively perfect in every way.

CHAPTER NINETEEN

MELANY

For the next few weeks, we were pushed harder in our training than ever before, and also introduced to new classes like swordplay, war strategy, potions and poisons, earth science, healing, and animal handling. The start of the trials was only two months away, and we needed to be ready to endure them.

No one was sure what the trials would entail, but we knew they weren't going to be easy. I'd heard a rumor we would be pitted against one or two of the demigods in a battle situation, and we'd have to use our training to survive. Hephaistos had let it slip one night, when I'd stayed late in the forge to put the final touches on my shield, that I'd be using the shield during the trials.

Thankfully, I didn't need to do the twelfth trial—Zeus's lightning—as I'd already suffered through a form of that one and passed—well, survived, would be a better term for what happened. I had daily reminders of that every time I looked in a mirror. Despite most everyone saying how cool the scars were, they reminded me of that night of the earthquakes and the devastation I'd seen. And my great loss.

During the weeks of training, I ducked outside to the maze every chance I got to see if Hades showed up again. But every time he wasn't there, more and more I came to the conclusion that Lucian had been right, and I'd imagined it due to overwork and stress. And I was definitely stressed, as we all were. Why my mind would conjure up the God of the underworld was beyond me. Why couldn't I imagine unicorns and rainbows?

"Oof." The blunted tip of Jasmine's sword struck me in the side. Again.

She frowned at me. "That's the third time I've gotten you. You're really distracted today."

Today? She was just being kind and not mentioning the day before when she'd knocked me on my ass with an overhead swing of the blunted sword. I'd moved too late and tripped over my own feet. Just about everyone in class had laughed at that. Including Ares. He laughed the loudest, as usual. His laugh was like a donkey's bray.

"Just thinking about the upcoming trials."

"Oh, I thought maybe you were thinking about the trips to the maze you make almost every day."

I pulled a face. "You know about that?"

"Yeah, Georgina and I followed you one time."

I should've known they would have.

"It always appears like you're looking for someone."

I shrugged. "No. Just taking some alone time."

Her eyebrows rose. "You sure you're not having romantic rendezvous with Lucian?"

She said his name loud enough that he turned and looked over at us.

My cheeks flared red. "I'm sure."

Except I was lying, and she likely knew I was lying, especially if she had followed me. Lucian and I had met up in the maze a few times and went flying together, always ending up on the balcony of the tallest tower to make out for an hour or so.

"Stop your chattering and do more sparring." Ares marched up to us, his brow furrowed in anger. "That's all you two do, talk, talk, talk." He made a flapping motion with his hand. "Talking isn't going to save you from a sword in the gut or a spear in the eye."

From nearby, I heard Revana's snicker.

"But it could save me from ever going to war in the first place." The moment I finished the last word, I knew I'd made a mistake.

Ares's face flushed beet red. He unsheathed the sword, his very real sword, at his waist and swung it toward my side. I drew up my shield just in time before his sword sliced off a nice thick chunk of my right flank. The tempered steel blade clashed against the metal of my shield. The sound reverberated through the gymnasium and vibrated over my skin.

He took a step back and swung quickly at my head. I blocked that blow, as well. Then he pivoted and thrust at me again. I blocked with my shield. The power of his blow traveled down my arm. He wasn't messing around.

Another thrust, jab, and overhead swing. I blocked them all, but barely. My arms ached from holding up the heavy shield and moving it to protect myself from being sliced in half. He came at me again and again, so hard and quick, that some of my peers were shouting at him to stop.

"Someone do something."

I heard Lucian's voice in the mix.

"Stop Ares! You're going to hurt her."

But he didn't stop. I'd obviously pushed him too far.

As he pivoted back on his foot to get another swing in, I dropped the shield to the side, formed a ball of fire in my hand, and threw it at him. He tried to duck out of the way, but the fire singed him across his arm. The sound of his skin crackling made my skin crawl. The stench filled my nose and my stomach roiled.

I stood there, gasping for breath, my heart pounding so hard my chest ached, glaring at him, and defying him to cut me down. I was through being a target of his vindictive anger.

But he didn't run me through with his sword. He met my gaze straight on and then gave me a curt nod. "Class dismissed."

I let out the breath I was holding, and nearly collapsed onto my knees, but I didn't want to give him the satisfaction.

Jasmine and Georgina were instantly at my side. Georgina took my shield.

"Holy crap. Are you okay?" Jasmine put her arm around me.

I nodded but had a feeling when the adrenaline stopped pumping through me, I was going to crash big time.

Mia joined us. "I can't believe he can do that. He almost killed you."

"Well, there's not anyone we can tell." Georgina shrugged. "It's not like we can call our parents. We don't have families anymore."

I looked at her. "We're family now. We have to look out for each other."

She nodded. "Can you be like the father of this family? You're way more in charge then I ever could be."

That made all of us laugh, as we made our way out of the gymnasium and back to the dorms. I caught Lucian's gaze on the way out, and he gave me a soft smile. It made my belly flutter, as his smiles always did.

Before we reached the dorms, Ren caught us. "Hey, I heard Dionysus is putting on a show in the north hall. Should be quite the party."

"Is this an academy sanctioned party?" Georgina asked.

Ren smirked. "Probably not. Which is why it's

going to be awesome." He slung an arm around my shoulders. "You of all people could use a good party. I mean, you almost died today. Again."

I snorted. "That's true."

After a quick shower and change of clothes, Georgina, Jasmine, and I met up with the others in the north hall. Music was already thumping before we even rounded the corner. As promised, Dionysus was DJing some epic beats, and there was food and drink a plenty, served by Hephaistos's little wooden robots on wheels. Laser lights danced around to the music.

I grabbed a plate of food and a drink and then commandeered a sitting area, which consisted of a sofa and bean-bag chair just off the makeshift dancefloor to eat. Georgina, Jasmine, Mia, Ren, and Marek joined me, all cramming in the space together. I looked around for Lucian but didn't see him. Disappointment flooded me. Despite our stolen moments in the maze, we hadn't had a lot of opportunity to socialize, especially in a group. I honestly didn't even know if he wanted people to know we were… I didn't even know what to call it. It's not like we were dating, the academy wasn't a place to date in. A relationship would've been too serious. I guess we were hanging out together. I really hoped he didn't want to hide that. I was already feeling pretty raw from the Ares incident I didn't want my whole heart torn out by Lucian's rejection.

After eating, Mia grabbed Jasmine's arm and pulled her out onto the dancefloor. I loved that Mia had been slowly urging Jasmine out of her shell. She'd been guarded before, but with Mia she let those walls down.

After watching them dance for a song, I couldn't resist getting out there myself, and I pulled everyone out there with me. We all deserved a chance to just let go and have some fun. It wouldn't be long before things got really serious and after the trials, some of us might even be kicked out if we didn't pass. There were twelve of them, and everyone had to pass at least eight to be considered for placement in a clan.

On the floor, I closed my eyes and let the music take over. Every thump of the bass oscillated through my body. It was like the music originated inside me. It was vibrant and exciting, and I couldn't stop smiling as I moved to the beat. Bodies pressed against mine, as we all jumped and gyrated. Then I felt a hand on my waist. Opening my eyes, I twirled around to find Lucian swaying his body next to me.

My grin nearly split my face it was so wide. Over-joyed he was here, I moved in closer to him and wrapped my arms around his neck. He settled his hands at my waist, and we danced together, our bodies in perfect rhythm. I knew we were getting looks, but I didn't care, and he didn't seem to, either.

We danced and laughed into the late hours. It was the best night of my life. When he ran off with Ren and a few others to check out Dionysus's music collection, I decided to duck out to get some air. Dionysus had used too much dry ice in the smoke machine, and it had clogged in my nose and throat.

I left the hall and stepped out into the main lobby. There were a few students gathered here and there in small groups. I moved around them, heading toward a small alcove containing a stone bench. But when I neared it, I realized it was occupied by Jasmine and Mia. They were sharing an intimate kiss. They both looked up as I approached.

"Oops, sorry." I put up my hand to excuse myself, making an abrupt right turn and out into the dark corridor nearby, smiling to myself. I was so happy Jasmine had found someone in this place.

I kept walking until I was alone and found a bench to sit on. I'd been there no more than five minutes before I heard footsteps as someone approached. Revana stepped into a pool of moonlight that radiated through one of the big arched windows high above.

"Did you actually follow me out here? That's a bit creepy, don't you think?"

"You think you're so clever."

I got to my feet. I had a feeling this wasn't just going to be a social call. "Yeah, pretty much."

"Lucian just feels sorry for you, you know? That's the only reason he's slumming it with you."

"Maybe." I shrugged. "But he's still with me and not you."

"For now." Her eyes narrowed. "I've had him before. I'll have him again. We were meant to be together."

"Whatever, Revana." I was going to have to pass by her to return to the hall. "Have your little fantasy.

Doesn't bother me any." I walked toward her with every intention of just brushing past her.

But she had other plans.

She grabbed my arm, turning me slightly. With her other hand, she tried to punch me in the face, but I sensed it coming and blocked her blow, countering with a strike to her midsection. It wasn't a hard blow, just a reminder to her that she shouldn't test me. I was better at hand to hand then she was.

"Walk away, Revana." I stepped back onto my left foot, preparing to fight if she provoked me any further. "This is a fight you won't win. I guarantee you that."

I thought for one moment, she was going to stand down, but then she flicked her wrist, and there was a small dagger in her hand. I didn't know where she'd had it stashed, but I knew she'd become proficient with knives, as she'd done some special training with Ares when he saw that she had an affinity to them.

"What? Are you going to kill me?"

"No, I'd get expelled for that." She spun the dagger expertly in her hand. "I'm just going to add to the ugly scars you already have."

She was skilled enough to wound me before I could disarm her. I had to find another way out of this. I cast my gaze around, sensing the shadows creeping along the walls and floor. I wasn't sure if I was doing it or someone else was, but soon we were cloaked in darkness.

"Coward!"

Revana's voice faded into the background, muffled

by the thick murkiness of the air.

Not completely confident of where I was going, I took a few steps to the left, hoping to pass by Revana and escape the corridor. After another few steps, I realized the ground beneath my shoes felt different. I was no longer walking on tile, but spongey grass.

I took another few steps forward and waved my hands in front of me. The shadows dissipated to reveal I was out in the center of the maze and not in the academy at all.

"Well done. I didn't think you'd be able to transport through the shadows, but you've proven me wrong."

I whipped around to see Hades sitting on the stone bench in the gazebo, as nonchalant as could be.

I walked toward him. "Did you bring me here?"

"I merely sent the darkness to you. You decided what to do with it."

Another thought popped into my mind. I remembered something Lucian had said to me before. "Did you save me from being electrocuted by Zeus's lightning?"

He tilted his head as he regarded me. "And what if I did? What would you say?"

I shrugged. "Thank you, I guess."

He laughed. "Yes, perfect." He stood and came toward me. "I like you, Melany. You have a lot of feistiness. It'll serve you well in the days to come."

"What days? What do you mean?"

Before he could answer, he stepped into a circle of darkness and sank into it, like quicksand, and vanished.

CHAPTER TWENTY

MELANY

I didn't tell anyone about the confrontation with Revana and the subsequent transporting through the shadows and talking with Hades in the maze. One, I didn't want to make the situation worse with Revana—besides that, I wasn't a snitch—and two, I didn't want to have to explain seeing Hades, a God who wasn't supposed to be allowed on school grounds. That would lead to too many questions, especially the one I didn't have an answer for—what was Hades's interest in me?

I put it all in the back of my mind as I buckled in for long, hard training. It was crunch time. We had only a couple of weeks until the trials.

Every day, I worked hard in my classes, even clocking in extra time in the evening before curfew, especially in animal handling class with Artemis and prophecy with Apollo, well, not directly with Apollo, but with Pythia, his assistant. I was having trouble wrangling and riding the fire-breathing horses in the stable. I'd had some luck with the griffin, and I once rode one of the unicorns, but the fire-breathing horses were the most powerful out of all the beasts. I wanted to learn how to tame them.

In prophecy class, Pythia helped me with divination. She told me that I'd never be able to do it until I learned to open myself up. During one extra practice, she'd tried to read into my past.

We sat across from one another in simple wooden chairs, knees touching. She held out her long, gnarled hands. "Take my hands."

I did, but not without wincing, as they felt like old, wrinkled leather. I felt bad, but I knew she couldn't see me. She was blind. She was self-conscious about her deformity, so she wore a gray blindfold around her face, where her eyes once were.

She clutched my hands, her twisted, claw-like nails digging into my skin. "You must learn to open your mind to others, so you in turn can see into theirs. You are too guarded."

I twisted my neck, the bones cracking from stiffness, and tried to relax. Closing my eyes, I attempted to empty my mind of all my worries, and there were many. I thought of calm water and light breezes. I imagined sitting in the garden back home listening to the chickadees chirp from the nearby trees.

"Relax your mind. If you can't, you will not pass the trial."

Her voice sounded far off as I started to drift. In my mind, I was floating on a sea of white, fluffy clouds. It was so peaceful, and I wondered if I could stay there awhile. But those fluffy clouds turned dark, and I shot downwards, landing on the ground. It was day, hot; the land looked like a desert wasteland. Then I saw a woman, a tall, slender, pretty woman with purple eyes. Her face was a mask of fear as she ran from a mob of people who wore robes and carried large stones.

The mob yelled at her as they chased her, calling her monster and witch. Then they started to throw the stones. She was hit in the body and head and face. Eventually, she stopped running as her legs gave out. On the ground, she tried to protect her head, as more stones flew at her. But she couldn't stop them from hitting her face. Blood poured down her cheeks to drip on the sand beneath her.

Opening my eyes, I gasped, realizing what I'd witnessed. The woman had been Pythia, and this was how she'd lost her eyes.

She squeezed my hands. "Yes. Good. Now open for me."

I pulled away from her memory and tried to empty my mind again to let her in.

I watched as her face contorted and twisted. Her brow furrowed deeply, her whole body twitching. She squeezed my hands so tight they hurt.

Then she cried out and flinched backward, nearly falling out of her chair.

"What is it?"

She shook her head and put a trembling hand to her chest. "You must go."

"Why? What happened? What did you see?"

"Please, just go."

I stood, but I needed to know. "What did you see? Please tell me."

"I saw nothing. Just darkness…"

That couldn't be all that bad. Maybe she just couldn't get into my past.

"And death."

A shiver rushed down my back, as I left the classroom. I didn't know what Pythia meant when she said death, but maybe she'd seen the destruction I'd seen on the trip back to Pecunia. That would've been a very strong memory for me.

When I returned to my dorm room, Georgina was already asleep. I crawled into bed and lay there, staring up at the ceiling. The whole thing had unnerved me. I wasn't sure I could sleep without seeing Pythia's past. But eventually, I got so tired I just passed out.

One day blurred into the next until it was time for the trials. I was excited but scared that I wasn't going to pass enough of them to be able to stay at the academy. I did have a slight advantage though, in that I only needed to pass seven more trials, as I'd already gone through the lightning ordeal. Despite not knowing what each trial entailed, I was confident I would pass anything to do with flying, fire, and hand-to-hand combat. I was pretty good with a bow now, and I could make a decent sleeping potion without killing anyone. I'd also proven myself in the water. It all depended on what we had to do in each trial. I suspected a few of them weren't going to be straight forward.

The night before the big day, we were allowed to spend it however we wanted to prepare. I spent it alone, walking through the maze. There was something about the place that settled my mind. It was like a kind of peace enveloped me. Maybe it was the darkness or the quiet. Whatever it was, I soaked it in as I sat inside the gazebo with my turbulent thoughts.

"So, I kind of feel like you're on my side somehow." I glanced around, hoping Hades would show. "Tomorrow is a huge day, and I'm… I'm afraid. I could really use a pep talk." I stood and walked over to the bench he'd perched on before. "Any words of wisdom? Any advice? A hug? I could use all of those things right about now." Laughing, I rubbed my hands over my face. "Mel, you are officially losing it."

"Who are you talking to?"

I whirled to see Lucian walking toward the gazebo. "No one. Myself, I guess." I shrugged.

He stepped up to me and grabbed my hand. "Do you want to go flying?"

"No." I shook my head. "Could you just hold me?"

He tugged me to him and wrapped his big arms around me, cuddling me close. I lay my head against his chest and inhaled, breathing the scent of him in. I was always surprised at how good he smelled. Like wood and pine, with just a touch of mint because of the gum he always chewed.

"You know, we might have to go against each other in the trials."

His hand on my back stilled. "I know."

"If given a choice, though, I won't fight against you. I'll pick someone else."

"Me too."

"I do hope I get a chance to fight Revana, though."

He chuckled and ran a hand over my head. "That I would love to see."

I raised my head to look at him. Going on my tiptoes, I brushed my lips against his. I couldn't think of a better way to spend the rest of the night—kissing Lucian until the sun started to pinken the sky and my lips got sore.

CHAPTER TWENTY-ONE

MELANY

*a*t 6 a.m., a trumpet-like horn sounded through the dorms.

It was a call to action.

I was already awake, having forgone sleep. I was wired and ready to go.

We all gathered in the great hall. Up on the dais, all twelve Gods looked out over their recruits. Zeus stepped forward to speak.

"Today marks the first day of the Trials. For the next twelve days, you will be engaged in the hardest tasks you've ever had to do thus far in your training. Each trial will last one day, and when you are not active in the trial, you will be in your dorm rooms resting. There will be no socializing, except with your dorm mates during the trials. Anyone caught outside of their dorm during rest time will be automatically expelled. No exceptions." His gaze landed directly on me.

He didn't have to worry; I had no plans to screw this up.

"These trials are created to best showcase the skills you've learned over the course of your training and to weed out the weak. Each trial is specialized to each God clan. How well you do in each of them will determine which clan you will be relegated to at the end of your first year here at the academy. To stay in the academy, you must pass no less than eight trials. Before each trial, you will be informed on what constitutes a pass and a failure. No two trials are the same in that regard."

Nerves vibrated through me. I hated I didn't know what to expect at each of the trials. It would be easier to know if we had to fight against each other, or against others. I could strategize better. As of right now, I didn't know what the hell I was going to do. But I supposed neither did anyone else. It put us all on a level playing field.

"You will be given specialized nourishment every day to keep your bodies strong and your minds sharp. I suggest you eat and drink what is given to you, as you will not have access to anything else throughout the twelve days.

"After your nourishment, which will be passed out shortly, meet out on the north training field at the sound of the horn.

"Good luck to all of you!"

He stepped back, and all of the Gods filed out of the room, as several of the serving robots rolled in, accompanied by Chiron and Heracles.

"Form three lines," Heracles bellowed.

We scrambled to get in the lines, as a protein bar and bottle of water were passed to each of us. I looked at the small bar and thought, *This is all we get?* I ate the bar; it tasted horrible but had a hint of cinnamon to make it at least edible. Then I washed it down with the water, which had a bitter tang to it.

After about five minutes, I started to feel a heat spread throughout my body. Eventually, my muscles felt stronger and bigger. My mind felt clearer. I smiled at Jasmine and Georgina, whose faces lit up with the same sensation I'd experienced.

"Damn. That's better than drugs."

The horn sounded, and we all exited the academy and gathered on the north training field as instructed. Hephaistos was there, waiting for us. All of our shields were resting up against a wooden rack like the one in the forge. Artemis stood beside him, as did Ares, albeit on the other side of Artemis. It was the first time I'd seen Hephaistos and Ares in the same area together.

"I'm not going to make some grand speech. It's pointless." Hephaistos hobbled forward. "You've essentially been training for this trial the entire time you've been in the forge. The shields you have created will be the determining factor whether you pass or not."

That sent a concerned murmur through the group.

"Shut it. If you hadn't already figured that out, you're stupid."

I couldn't stop the bubble of laughter erupting. Both Jasmine and Georgina whipped their heads around and gaped at me.

"Melany Richmond," Hephaistos bellowed. "You may as well step forward and get this trial started."

Oh shit.

A path was made for me, and I stepped out from the group and onto the field.

Ares smirked and shook his head.

"Grab your shield."

I ran to the rack, found my shield, and attached it to my arm. I looked at Hephaistos for the rest of the instructions.

"Now don't get hit."

I looked around wildly. "From what?"

Artemis raised her arms, her bow strung with a long, sharp arrow. Fire erupted between Hephaistos's hands. Ares unsheathed his sword.

Oh shit.

"Start at the end of the field and run back here. If you can make it without being hit by an arrow, struck by a sword, or burned by fire, with your shield intact, you'll pass."

I ran as fast as I could down the field. Once I reached the end where a red flag was planted, I took a deep breath, made sure my shield was secure, and then ran toward the chaos.

I hadn't even taken two steps before two arrows

rained down on me. I blocked them both, the arrowheads pinging off my shield, and continued on. A fireball came next. It hit my shield, exploded, but I was safe behind it. All that sizzled were the ends of my hair.

I kept pressing forward. More arrows came; I blocked them from hitting me in the legs and arms and head. Other fireballs also soared through the air toward me. Some hit the ground where I'd just been, and others exploded over my shield. Then they came at the same time, and I had to do some fancy maneuvering and dodging, so I didn't get an arrow through the shoulder and a fireball at my head. Hearing my friends cheering me on buoyed my step, and I kept running even faster.

As I got closer to the finish line, Ares came sprinting out toward me, his sword arched back. He swung at me, and I blocked it with my shield. He swung at me again, and again, and again. I had a sense he was going a little harder on me.

I blocked his next hard overhead blow and then pushed up with my shield, shoving him off balance. I sprinted like a cheetah to the finish line. When I crossed it, just about everyone cheered. Hephaistos greeted me and took my shield to inspect it.

Ares stormed back, his face beet red. "She cheated! She should fail!"

Hephaistos didn't even acknowledge him but continued to inspect the integrity of the metal of my shield. He nodded. "Not a dent. Congratulations, you passed."

Ares sputtered. "She cheated. I'm going to bring it up to—"

Hephaistos's large, beefy hand around Ares's throat stopped his words. "Don't tell me how to run my trial." Then he shoved the God of War away.

Still red-faced, almost purple really, Ares stormed off the training field. I didn't know what stunned me more: that Hephaistos had moved so fast and bested Ares, or that Ares had left without a fight.

Hephaistos shrugged. "Guess someone else will be swinging the sword."

I laughed, as did a bunch of others. We were rewarded with a quick but potent grin from the craftsman God.

Breathing a sigh of relief that I'd finished and passed trial one, I stayed and cheered on my friends and the rest of my peers. I even lost myself and clapped when Revana made it through the gauntlet virtually unscathed. It was a good day, as no one failed the trial.

The next day, we all gathered in the garden near the hedge maze. Demeter welcomed us there in her usual laid-back manner. It was a nice reprieve from all the tension from the day before.

"I imagine y'all are thinking that I'm going to put you through some impossible feat." She shook her head. "Nah, man, I don't believe in all that bullshit."

There were some sighs of relief from people and some nervous giggles. I looked at Jasmine and Georgina and saw the same looks of relief on their faces. Especially Georgina. She'd passed through

Hephaistos's trial, but it hadn't been easy for her, and she had suffered a bit of a burn on her arm from one of his fireballs.

"So, your task today is to get into teams of five and make it through the maze."

I laughed. This was going to be too easy. I could walk the maze with my eyes closed.

"But…" This quieted some of the excited murmurs. "I did redesign the maze. I mean, I wasn't going to make it *that* easy for you miscreants."

Everyone laughed at that.

"Oh, but you are being timed." Demeter grinned. "You'll have twenty minutes to get through it to the center. Get into groups!"

Jasmine, Georgina, and I stuck together. Ren jumped over to our group, and Jasmine grabbed Mia and pulled her in. I looked over at Lucian. He met my gaze and gave me a smile. I wasn't worried about him. He was smart, and he was in a driven, competitive group who wouldn't fail.

Lucian's group entered first. I was nervous waiting, hoping his team went through all right. After about fifteen minutes, Demeter clapped. "All right, who's next?"

We jumped to the front of the line.

"On your mark, get set, and go!"

We went into the maze together, took an immediate right, and kept walking. Then we came to an intersection. I was about to suggest right when a tiny arrow flashed on the ground, showing us the way. I laughed.

Demeter really did hate all of this stuff, and I wondered if she would get in trouble from Zeus for it.

No more than fifteen minutes later, we came out into the middle of the maze. The other group was still there, and they were happily munching on pastries and cookies and all kinds of other tasty foods. When Lucian spotted me, he rushed over and offered me a plate of chocolate cupcakes.

"I was hoarding them for you."

I took one, peeled the wrapper, and shoved it into my mouth. I grinned at him around it.

For the rest of the day, we all chilled out in the middle of the giant hedge maze with our friends and peers and ate as many desserts as we could all fit into our mouths. Because we all knew we wouldn't get another reprieve like this. Things were just starting to get hard.

The next morning after eating the allocated protein bar and drinking the water, it was Dionysus's turn to challenge us. We met in his lab, where we'd been learning how to make different types of potions and tinctures, some of them for healing, others for more mischievous purposes.

"Good morning, my little apothecaries." His speech was a bit slurred, and I wondered if he was drunk already. Or hadn't stopped being drunk. Maybe drunk was his natural state of being. It was hard to tell.

"For this great trial, you will need to create three different potions." He ticked them off on his fingers. "Sleeping potion, super strength, and invisibility. Now since you've been learning to make these all term, you won't be provided with a recipe. You must make it on your own. All the ingredients for each potion can be found here in the workshop. You have two hours to complete your potions."

Before everyone could scatter to collect ingredients, Dionysus held up his finger.

"Once you've crafted your potions, you will be testing them on someone else. And I get to pick that someone else," he said with aplomb. "To pass this trial, at least two out of the three potions need to work properly. And if you end up poisoning someone, I won't be held responsible." He smiled and waved his hand in the air. "Begin."

While there was a mad rush for the valerian root— obviously everyone was starting with their sleeping potion, which was the easiest recipe to remember and to make—I opted for the ginseng. I was going to tackle the super strength potion first. Then for my sleeping potion, I was going to base it in lemon balm and not valerian, which was the more volatile herb.

I took my time making my potions, as quality was the important factor here. Every now and then, I peeked at my fellow recruits to see how they were fairing. I knew both Jasmine and Georgina were competent potion makers, so I didn't worry about them. Ren looked a bit flustered, as did Lucian. If either of them were going to fail at any trial, it would be this one or one of the other cerebral ones. I had no doubt that they would both excel in the more physically exerting trials.

Two hours passed quickly. Dionysus blew a whistle, and we all had to stop.

"Okay, now to test them." He walked around the workroom, peering at everyone's potions. He stopped at Jasmine's station. "You can test yours on…" His gaze traveled the room and then he grinned, pointing at me. "Melany. And vice versa."

Jasmine and I both picked up our individual vials and walked them to the front of the classroom to set them on the front table in the holders.

"Let's start with the super strength."

I handed Jasmine my potion and I took hers. I looked at her, and on the count of three, we both drank. It tasted like licorice, and I wondered if she'd added that for flavor.

"Now to test it." Dionysus pointed to the iron anvil sitting in the corner.

Jasmine and I walked over to it. "You first," she said.

I crouched, put my hands around it, and easily lifted the four hundred pound anvil. I grinned at Jasmine. Then it was her turn, and she also easily lifted it. That was one down, now onto the invisibility potion.

We drank at the same time, and within seconds we both faded from view. It was really cool to watch, knowing I'd brewed that. The effects only lasted for a few minutes; Dionysus had us design it that way. Later, we would learn how to make one that would last for hours.

"Now, technically, you both passed, but I want to see how you did with the sleeping potion." He pointed to two chairs in the corner.

We sat, and both of us downed the other's potion. I was happy to taste that Jasmine had used the lemon balm as well. That was the last coherent thought I had until sometime later Dionysus nudged us awake to find that Mia, Ren, and Diego hadn't passed. Ren's invisibility potion had turned Revana green. Literally. If I hadn't been sad that he hadn't passed the trial, I would've laughed my ass off at that.

Later that night, I lay in my bed and stared up at the ceiling, hoping I had the strength and fortitude to continue on. I'd passed four trials; I just needed to pass four more to stay at the academy. I couldn't be cast out. I wouldn't survive that. I was worried about tomorrow's trial, as it was with Apollo and Pythia. I hadn't done well in practice with Pythia. I hoped that it didn't hamper my performance.

Apollo paired us up the next day, with the intention of reading each other. I was hoping for someone I'd be comfortable with, someone I could open up to. I got Revana.

We sat in chairs facing each other, forced to touch knees.

"You must each read something from each other's past and say it out loud. Those who do not extract that information won't pass the trial." Apollo touched us both on the heads. "Clasp hands."

Resigned to my fate, I offered mine, and Revana slapped hers into my palms. I wrapped my fingers around her hands and squeezed. Probably harder than I needed to, but I didn't care. I wanted to pass this trial, and I wasn't going to let her mess with that.

I closed my eyes, took in a deep breath, and concentrated on Revana. I focused on her hands in mine, the sound of her breathing, the scent of vanilla she always carried on her. Then I shot into her mind, into one of her strongest memories. I hated that I had to speak it out loud. It was an invasion of privacy in the worst way.

"I'm at a track meet. Revana is racing; she looks maybe eleven or twelve."

Revana's hands tightened on mine, and I could feel her pulse thudding hard in her wrist.

"The gun goes off, and Revana sprints down the lane. She's running hard. she's passing the other girls. She's almost at the finish line, when another girl comes from behind and crosses first."

I didn't want to continue. Even in the memory, I could feel Revana's disappointment. Her despair. Her hatred at herself for losing the race.

"She's coming into her house, her parents entering behind her. She turns to look at her father. He doesn't smile at her. She tells him she's sorry. He scowls at her, and tells her she's stupid..."

Opening my eyes, I stopped and shook my head. I didn't want to go on.

"You have to tell us everything you see, Melany, if you want to pass this trial."

Revana glared at me and dug her fingernails into the backs of my hands. "Just do it."

"He tells her she's stupid and worthless. No one cares about second place. First place is the only thing in life that's important. She says she's sorry again. He slaps her across the face." I sighed. "That's it. That's the end of the memory."

Apollo nodded. "Good. Your turn, Revana."

I took in another cleansing breath, trying to relax and open for her. I hated that she was going to be poking around in my head, but it had to happen for the sake of the trial. I didn't have any way of blocking her. She was going to see what she was going to see. I had no control over what memory she plucked from my subconscious.

Revana stared into my eyes, as she squeezed my hands tighter. I was going to have divots in my skin. Her eyes narrowed, and her breathing picked up. "I can't see anything." She yanked on my hands. "Let me in."

"I am." And I was. Or at least, I think I was. I wasn't actively blocking her.

She snapped her eyes shut, and her face contorted in concentration.

"Try harder, Revana," Apollo said from next to us.

"I am."

"You only have a few more minutes to complete the task."

I wanted to tell him to shut up; he wasn't helping.

Finally, her eyes flicked open, and she pulled her hands away. "Nothing. I couldn't see anything."

Apollo frowned. "You couldn't capture one memory?"

"There was nothing there to capture. Her mind was just dark."

He glanced down at me. "Were you blocking her?"

I stood. "No, of course not. I wouldn't know how to do that, even if I wanted to."

"Okay, you pass, Melany. I'm afraid, Revana, you failed this trial."

"You bitch!" Revana bolted to her feet and sucker punched me right in the mouth then she stomped out of the room.

Shaking his head, Apollo glanced at Pythia and shrugged. "I have a feeling this is going to be a long day."

The way Pythia looked at him, I thought for sure she was going to say something about the other day when the same thing had happened to her. But she didn't.

Later in the dorm room, Georgina asked me, "What did you do to Revana? She came out of the room with smoke blowing out of her nose. She said you were going to pay."

I shrugged. "I didn't do anything. She didn't pass the trial and blamed me for it." I collapsed onto my bed and turned toward the wall, tucking my legs up. I didn't want to talk about what had happened to anyone.

Today was a hard day, and I knew it was just going to get even harder. Right now, we weren't being pitted against each other much, but I knew it was coming. Today, it was Revana, what if tomorrow it was Georgina, or Jasmine, or even Lucian? Could I protect my friends while I protected myself? I really hoped so because I didn't want to face the alternative.

CHAPTER TWENTY-TWO

MELANY

*B*efore heading into the hall of Aphrodite for our next trial, Lucian caught me and pulled me aside.

"Are you okay?"

"Yeah, I'm good."

He lifted his hand and touched my puffy, sore lip. Revana's fist had split it open. "What happened? The rumor is you cheated or something, causing Revana to fail the trial."

I lifted an eyebrow. "And what do you think?"

"I think that's bullshit."

"Exactly." I beamed at him, happy he didn't believe the stupid rumor.

He smiled and tugged me close for a quick hug.

"How did you do in the trial?"

He hugged me tighter. "Not good. I didn't pass it."

I pulled back and looked him in the eyes. "I'm sorry."

He shrugged. "It's one fail. I don't plan on failing any others."

Aphrodite looked like a gold statue, as she stood on her little dais in her hall and addressed us. "My trial is one of deception. Over the past few months, you've learned how to transform your body into something else. From human to animal. For this trial, you will transform yourself into a goat."

That got a few snickers from the group.

"The object of this will be for your peers to pick you out of a herd of goats. If they do, you fail. In the old days, we would've slaughtered the goats one by one to reveal your identity, but we won't be doing that here."

I shared a horrified look with Jasmine. "Yikes."

Half of the group was escorted out of the room, while the rest of us stayed. So when the door opened again, and ten goats came scampering in, we didn't know whom it was that had transformed into a goat right away. It was smart to do that because it was possible that someone could still retain some defining feature, like a mole or a scar.

Our goal as a group was to examine each goat and then make a unanimous decision on which goat wasn't really a goat. I didn't have to voice my thoughts, but I was sure we all pretty much agreed not to out anyone if we spotted any obvious discrepancies in goats. This was one time when we could help out our peers.

After we all looked over the ten goats, we came together and made a decision. We agreed on picking the all-white goat. Jasmine was our spokes person.

She pointed to the white goat. "We think that one is an imposter."

Aphrodite nodded. "Very well."

She then snapped her fingers, and eight of the goats turned back into our peers, including the one we'd picked. The goat turned out to be Lucian.

My stomach churned. I stared at him in horror.

Aphrodite stepped off the dais and moved toward us. Her gaze flashed with blue fire. "Don't mess with me." She then gestured to the students picking themselves off the ground. "You all passed, except for you, dear." She pointed to Lucian. "You failed, thanks to your friends here."

Wow. Aphrodite was a real nasty piece of work. I was going to have to watch her more closely.

We took more care with the next group of goats that came in and thankfully didn't pick anyone. When it was my turn to transform, I did it as quick as I could, hoping that I did it well. There were no mirrors around, so I couldn't take a look at myself and fix any issues. Other goats joined me in the lobby; I didn't know if they were actually goats or my friends. The doors opened and we all ran into the room.

I tried to be as goat-like as I could. I made goat noises and butted my head into another goat, which I hoped was an actual animal and not one of my friends. Revana and her crew were part of the observing party. As she moved through the herd, she kicked at each animal. After seeing what I did from her past, I wanted to feel sorry for her, but the truth was she was not a good person.

When she neared me, she booted me in the side. Pain rippled over my body, and I wanted to whip my head around and nip her in the ass, but I didn't. Instead, I bleated at her and moved along to stand next to a little brown goat.

After a few tense moments of the group conferring, Revana pointed to a medium-sized black and white goat. "That's not a goat."

Aphrodite nodded and then snapped her fingers. Me, Jasmine, Georgina, Ren, and Mia all popped into existence. As did Ren's roommate Marek, but he'd been the one they'd pointed out. He'd failed the trial.

That night in the dorm, Georgina told me how scared she was for the rest of the trials.

"I've passed five of them, but I still need to pass three more, and I'm afraid I won't be able to as they're going to be the more physical ones."

"You're strong, Gina. Stronger than I think you even know." I grabbed her hand. "And if I can help you during any of the trials, you know I will."

Once more, my sleep wasn't all that good. I had dreams this time, of darkness and shadows. And I wondered if it was some kind of portent of things to come.

Hera's trial was very much like a locked room adventure. I'd done one with Callie and her friends. Everyone had spent the time arguing, so we never made it out. For the trial, we'd be in a group of five, and we had to use our knowledge of the Gods to uncover clues inside a room to discover another door, to move on to the next room. We had to clear three rooms in an hour. The team with the worst timed score failed the trial.

We got into our usual group, me, Jasmine, Georgina, and Mia. Ren decided to go into another group with Marek to make sure he didn't fail another trial, which made room for a new member to our group —Lucian. I was confident that our group would make it through the rooms in record time, as everyone had done well in history class. I was probably the weakest link this time.

Once we were locked in the room, I grabbed Lucian's hand. "I'm so sorry for yesterday."

He shook his head. "Don't be. It's okay."

"But you failed—"

"I won't fail anymore. Especially not this one." He gave me a soft smile.

Together, we worked through the puzzles in record time. At least we thought it was record time, as we didn't know the other teams' scores. After every group finished going through the rooms, we found out that we had come in second place. Ren's team had come in first, which I was very happy to hear. Revana's team came in last. That meant she had two fails so far.

Not that I was celebrating. Okay, maybe I was just a little.

That night, I slept long and hard. I needed it to be fresh for Hermes's flying trial. I had no doubt that Lucian and I would do well, but I couldn't count out running into problems. Problems like Revana and her crew. It was no secret that the word in the halls was that they were out to get me. I had to watch my back.

Hermes met us out on the training field. He wore a blue polka dotted bow tie today, which I thought was really cute.

"This trial will be a race. Since flying is a fundamental part of your training as a soldier, only the first twenty-five flyers will pass this trial. The other half of the group will fail."

I glanced at Georgina and Jasmine. We all knew that the trials were going to get tougher. This was just an example of that. I was worried for Georgina. She was not a strong flyer.

"You will race in five heats of ten flyers. The best times will advance; the worst times will fail. I will pick the flyers for each heat."

I quickly moved away from my friends, hoping Hermes didn't just put a group together by proximity. I didn't want to race against them. Despite my tactic of moving around, I ended up in a group with Lucian, Ren, Marek, Mia, Revana, Diego, and three others I didn't know well.

After Hermes described the race route, we lined up on the starting line on the ground. Part of the trial was how fast we could produce our wings and shoot into the air. Thank the Gods, Lucian and I had done a lot of practicing.

Hermes stood in front of us, his arms raised. Then he dropped them, shouting, "Go!"

My big, black wings popped out of my back in seconds, and I was air born. Lucian was right behind me, with Revana, Ren, and Mia shortly behind him. The others took a little longer to get their wings out, and then they flew into the air.

It was now a game of follow-the-leader, and I was in front. Lucian kept up but stayed a little behind me, and I wondered if he was protecting my back from Revana because I knew she was going to come for me given half the chance. In the air away from prying eyes was the perfect opportunity.

I soared past the first spire over the citadel and was swooping around the north towers when I risked taking glancing behind me. Lucian was still on my tail, but Revana had gained some ground. She was wing to wing beside Mia. Ren was a little bit behind them.

She must've known I was checking for her position because she edged in closer to Mia, her wing flapping against the other girl's. She was trying to knock Mia out to get my attention. Well, it was working. I slowed my pace a little, intending to drop back, but Lucian saw what I was planning and shook his head. He came up beside me.

"Don't play into her games. Keep flying."

I looked over my shoulder again to see Revana violently bumping into Mia. I wasn't having it.

"You take the lead." I could afford to fail a trial. I folded my wings in and dropped back like a shot to where Revana and Mia flew. Revana's eyes nearly bugged out when she saw me.

"You want to mess with me, mess with me, not with my friends." I shot out my wings and did a spin around her. The force of it knocked her off balance, and she fell behind. I nodded to Mia. "Get in front of me."

She did, and we flew in a triangle formation, Lucian in the lead, Mia, then me and Ren along the side. Revana was right on my tail, but my huge wing flaps were too forceful for her to fight against. She couldn't get any speed around me.

By the time we flew around the towers and back to the finish line, Lucian was already touching down. He crossed first, then Mia, Ren, me, and Diego had managed to come in alongside with Revana, and Laura, one of the girls I didn't know well. Marek came in then the other two.

I didn't know what our times were, but for sure Lucian and Mia had the fastest times. I was fairly certain I'd be okay, but it all depended on how the other heats went.

Nervously, we watched the other groups fly. Jasmine did really well in the second heat, and I was sure she'd pass. Georgina, on the other hand, came in seventh in her heat.

After all the races finished, Hermes had us line up

again then he told us the results. I'd been right—
Lucian and Mia had the fastest times. I'd passed, as did
Ren, Jasmine, and Revana. But Georgina and Marek
had failed the trial. I think that was number three for
Marek and two for Georgina. I was going to have to
keep an eye on her during the next few trials. There
was no way I was going to let her get kicked out of the
academy.

CHAPTER TWENTY-THREE

MELANY

Georgina and I huddled in our room and talked for the rest of the afternoon and evening. She was upset she'd failed the flying trial, but I assured her that I wouldn't let her fail anymore. We talked about our pasts and our families and about boys. She told me about the boy back home that she'd left behind, and I told her about Lucian.

"Are you in love with him?" She nudged me playfully with her foot, as we sat on her bed.

"I honestly don't know." But I did know. And I was. I just didn't want to say it out loud because I didn't know what it truly meant here in the academy, especially during the trials. Love and friendship were complicated constructs, especially at a time when getting ahead meant leaving others behind.

In the morning as we assembled to get our meal for the day, I palmed my protein bar and when no one was looking, I gave it to Georgina.

Her eyes widened, and she shook her head. "I can't take this."

"Take it and eat it. I don't need it, Gina. I can afford to lose." I moved away from her, so she couldn't give it back. I peered over my shoulder and was satisfied to see she ate it.

Out on the south training field next to the stables, Artemis greeted us on top of one of the great fire-breathing horses that no one thus far had been able to ride. The beast snorted and stamped its big hooves against the dirt, making us all flinch backward.

"In this trial, you will wrangle one of the great beasts and ride them out here to the obstacle course." She gestured to the field, where a track had been created, including jumps and other hurdles. "There are ten targets. You must hit eight of them with your bow. Missing more than two is an automatic fail. You will also be timed, so even if you make all the required targets, you can't be slow. The best times and targets of the best twenty-five will pass. The rest will fail."

There were quite a few groans in the group, as well as a few very concerned looks. A couple of people were already sitting on their third fail.

"Get into two lines."

We all scrambled to do as she asked, but I didn't like it.

"I forgot to add that you will be racing against each

other but through opposite ends of the course." She pointed to the line I was in. "You head through the course from here." She pointed to the beginning of the track. "And this line will start from here." She gestured to the end.

I looked across from me to see whom I'd be racing against. Isobel glared at me. I nodded. It was a good choice. She was no threat to me. She could barely ride. During class, she'd fallen off every mount she tried.

I looked behind me to see who Georgina's opponent was and my heart sank. Revana would try everything she could to win. I wouldn't put it past her to cheat. I turned, grabbed Georgina, and switched places with her.

"Trust me," I whispered in her ear.

Artemis rode her horse in a path between our two lines. "Look across from you. This is whom you will be racing against."

I turned my head and gave Revana a huge, smug grin.

We were four back in line, so it was going to be an hour or more before we raced, but I knew the time would go by quick. And watching the others race wasn't at all boring. Lucian was two ahead of me. Before it was his turn, he turned around and gave me a quick smile. I returned it and gave him a lame thumbs up, which made him laugh. I checked to see whom he was racing against, Hella who wasn't very good at animal handling, and relaxed. Lucian was by far the most formidable one in the group.

When Artemis blew her whistle, Lucian grabbed the bow and quiver of arrows from the ground and sprinted into the stable. He was a millisecond behind his opponent. A few minutes later, Hella rode out on a unicorn. Unicorns were swift creatures; they could sprint faster than all the other horses. Another few seconds ticked by and I wondered what was taking Lucian so long.

Then he burst out through the large hole in the stable roof on Pegasus. Throughout our training, he'd been one of the only ones who the winged horse liked. Everyone else couldn't even get within a few feet of her.

Everyone broke out into cheers and whoops as the big beast swooped toward the obstacle course. Even Artemis grinned as Lucian made easy work of the course. He was back before Hella, missing only one target.

When he landed and dismounted, Artemis nodded to him. "Well done."

"Thank you." He awarded the group with an arrogant bow.

I shook my head and laughed. It felt good to laugh, especially now.

When it was my turn, my heart pounded so hard in my chest I could barely breathe. The whistle blew, and I picked up the bow and arrows and ran for the stable. Revana and I were neck and neck. She went straight for one of the griffins; I'd seen her practice with them, but along the way she kicked at all the other stall doors, which sent the occupants into a tizzy.

As she mounted her griffin, I couldn't even get near the other beasts. The unicorns were flailing their heads, their horns now a lethal weapon. The other griffins were stamping and snorting, clawing the air with their giant talons. I could forget about the Pegasus; she'd put her back to me, and I wasn't about to approach her. The fire-breathing horses were all skittish, some blowing smoke out of their nostrils. That left one beast —one of the fire-breathing horses, the biggest of them. His name was Aethon, and he was Ares's personal mount.

He stood there staring at me, his tail swishing back and forth, as if he didn't have a care in the world. He was huge; my head didn't even come up to his back.

"What do you think there, handsome? Want to go for a ride?"

He snorted, smoke curling out from his nostrils, but then he shifted just slightly, giving me access to his back. I couldn't believe it.

I ran toward him, jumped, grabbed a handful of long, black mane and mounted him. Then he was out of the stable like a thundering storm cloud. I heard a collective shout and gasp from the crowd, as I rode the huge beast to the obstacle course. We had some ground to cover, as Revana had already started through the course.

I sat up high on the horse, aimed and hit the first target, which was high in a tree, even before we entered the circuit. Aethon made short work of the jump over the logs then I hit the next target, which was low on the ground. As I rode through the sparsely wooded course, I could hear the squawks and wings flapping of Revana's griffin. Despite the griffin's speed and agility, I knew she was going to have a hard time because of its vast wingspan. It wouldn't be able to get as low as she'd want it to be for a few of the targets. Lucian wouldn't have had a problem with the Pegasus because she was also a horse and was comfortable on the ground, whereas the griffin was clumsier on the ground than in the air.

After hitting six targets straight on, we rounded the corner and ran into Revana and the griffin. It screeched at me, but Aethon wasn't concerned. He kept to the trail, thundering down it like a locomotive. I didn't think anything would stop him, let alone some angry griffin and an even angrier girl upon its back.

I hit the seventh target, which was precariously close to where Revana hovered.

"You could've hit me!"

"But I didn't."

She knocked her arrow in her bow, drew it, and swung around toward me. I looked around, but there was no target close to me.

"You're going to waste your arrow."

Her glare sharpened. "It won't be a waste." She let it fly.

The arrow whizzed by my head. I could feel the displacement of the air, and the sound of it buzzed in my ears. I knew she was angry. I knew she wanted to see me fail. But to actually want to kill me? I didn't think she had it in her. Obviously, I'd been wrong.

Aethon wasn't having it. That arrow could've hit him, too. He reared up, and blew a stream of fire from his mouth. Flames tickled the tips of the griffin's hooves, and he reared back, swooping to the right, and Revana nearly fell off his back.

As we galloped past her, I turned and flipped her the middle finger.

Aethon snorted, and I almost swore he chuckled.

I hit the last of the targets, not missing one, and then we thundered out of the course and back to the finish line. I was greeted to some claps and cheers. Revana flew in a few minutes behind.

After I dismounted, Aethon snorted then nuzzled my head from behind, knocking me off balance. Then he trotted back into the stables on his own.

Artemis brought her horse alongside me. "No one has ever ridden Aethon before."

"Don't tell Ares," I said.

She grinned. "I won't."

As Revana brushed past me, I grabbed her arm and leaned into her. "Don't push me, Revana. I'll let this one go because of what happened in prophecy, but next time… I will retaliate."

She jerked out of my grip and stomped away.

Georgina was next to race. I hugged her. "Good luck. Take a unicorn, the griffins are too hard to maneuver."

She nodded then the whistle blew. She sprinted into

the stable. A minute later, she rode out on a unicorn, and it sprinted toward the course. She was ahead of Isobel by a few seconds, who came out on one of the griffins. Within seconds, she fell off and had to scramble up onto the beast's back. But the griffin wasn't having it, and it flew away to return to the stable.

Isobel let out an exasperated scream.

Artemis rode up to her. "Do you wish to try another mount?"

She shook her head. She knew it was pointless. Her time would've been bad and she'd fail anyway.

"You've forfeited. You're an automatic fail."

When Georgina rode back in, she was all smiles. I hugged her after she dismounted. "Yeah, I'm so proud of you."

"I wouldn't have done it without you."

Arm in arm, we stood back and watched as Jasmine made her run. She rode out of the stable on one of the fire-breathing horses and sped toward the course. When she returned in great time, she wasn't happy.

"I missed three targets."

"Oh, Jas, I'm sorry." I hugged her. "But it's only one trial. You got the rest." I gave her a reassuring smile, but I wasn't so sure about Poseidon's trial. She was pretty good in the water, but I'd heard rumors the water God was infamous for his difficult tests.

After everyone went through the course, Artemis let us know the results. I'd placed first, with Lucian a few seconds behind. Georgina, Ren, and Mia had passed.

Revana had passed but barely. Isobel failed, and Diego was part of the twenty-five who had failed.

It was getting close to the end. We only had four trials left—Poseidon, Ares, Zeus, and the last one was for Athena. These ones were going to push us to the limits of our abilities. I was afraid, not for me, but for my friends. I didn't want to lose them. They were all I had left in this world.

CHAPTER TWENTY-FOUR

MELANY

*a*s I stood on the shore of the lake—that Lucian and I had discovered during one of our flights around the grounds—with my friends beside me, I couldn't stop shaking. I wasn't scared, well not entirely, but had adrenaline racing through me in anticipation of the trial. We all wore red and black wetsuits with the option of wearing goggles. I opted to wear them, as did Jasmine and Georgina. I noticed that both Ren and Lucian went without.

Poseidon stood proudly in front of us, the water of the lake lapping at his bare feet.

"This trial will test all your limits. This is a four-mile wide lake, and you will have three hours to swim from here to the opposite shore. There is a rest station in the middle for those who need it, but remember that you are competing against your peers. The first twenty-five swimmers to hit the opposite beach pass this trial. The rest will fail."

I glanced at my friends. This was it; this was going to be a real test. But I wasn't going to leave any of them behind. I reached for Lucian's hand and tugged him closer. Frowning, he looked down at me.

"No matter what, don't stop for me."

"Blue…"

"I mean it. You need to pass this trial. Please just concentrate on that." I squeezed his hand. "Promise me."

After a few seconds, he nodded. "Okay, I promise."

I let go of his hand, turning my attention back on Poseidon.

"You may use your skills however you see fit during this trial." A slow smile spread across his face. "But remember, you aren't alone in the water."

About fifteen feet out, the normally tranquil surface rippled. A small fin breeched the water, then another, then another, until there were nine small fins sticking out from the surface. There was more bubbling then the fins disappeared.

Jasmine grabbed my arm; her hands were trembling. "That's a hydra." Her voice was barely audible over the splashing of the lake water onto the beach.

"Are you sure? It didn't look very big."

"Those fins were just one of many on the tops of their heads."

I swallowed. Dealing with a baby Charybdis had

been nothing compared to the possibility of a one hundred foot sea dragon with nine heads.

Taking Jasmine with me, I huddled in next to Georgina, Lucian, and Ren. Jasmine grabbed Mia and pulled her into the group. "We need to stay together as much as we can. I have a feeling there's going to be strength in numbers."

Everyone nodded. Then Poseidon blew into his shell horn to start the race.

We all entered the water, trying to stay close together. It was going to be a long swim, but I was sure if we grouped our strengths, we could all make it to the other beach and pass the trial. I knew Ren and Lucian had two fails, so I didn't expect or want them to sacrifice their time for us, well, for me in particular.

Once in the water, Ren and Lucian set the pace, and the rest of us followed behind. I sucked in air, then dived down to swish my body back and forth like a fish, propelling myself forward. Everyone else did the same; then we surfaced and did it again.

The next time I came up for air, I did quick look behind and saw we were making good time, and we were middle of the pack. It was a good position to be, as we could put on the speed at the end.

After about an hour of swimming, my muscles started to ache and fatigue was trying to settle into my body. I looked over at Georgina; she was struggling a bit. I swam over to her.

"Next time we dive down, hang onto my foot and just glide with me."

"Are you sure?"

"Yup."

She nodded, and we both took in air and dove. As instructed, she grabbed my foot, as I propelled my body forward like a dolphin. I didn't go as far or as fast, but it helped her conserve energy, so I considered it worthwhile. We did it again and again, until my legs started to seize up.

We swam close to the floating rest station. I saw a couple of people scramble up onto it to rest. In theory, it seemed like a good idea, but I knew from experience they couldn't rest enough to make a difference in their muscles when they got back into the water. Oxygen wise it was sound, but I suspected those people were going to suffer some severe cramps during the next half of the journey.

Halfway there and I felt optimistic. Ren and Lucian led the way, and they hadn't slowed. Like a flock of birds, we were conserving energy by swimming in the current they made with their bodies. I looked back. We'd pulled away a little from the pack. There were a few people swimming at our rate, and there was one person—I think it was Marek, judging by his black hair —who was ahead of us.

As the shore came into view, I started to smile, but a shout from someone nearby nearly froze me in place.

"I felt it under me!" It was Diego, and he thrashed about back and forth.

"Quit moving around," Revana shouted, as she moved away from Diego. "You'll draw it to us."

"It's not a shark. It's a freaking hydra. I think it's going to do what it wants."

Another shout came from another group of people.

Georgina started to thrash a little beside me. I shook my head. "Don't panic. Just concentrate on your strokes. We're almost there."

Then Diego was yanked down into the water.

That made everyone within a ten-foot radius scream.

Georgina was one of them.

"Lucian!"

He stopped swimming and turned to me. "What happened?"

"Something happened to Diego."

Ren swam over. "What do you want to do?"

"Can you take Georgina, Jasmine, and Mia with you? Swim to the shore."

He frowned. "Mel… he wouldn't do it for you."

"I know."

He shook his head and looked at Lucian. "You take the girls. I'm going to go with Mel."

"No, he's my friend—"

"I can manipulate the water. Mel and I can hold our breath the longest."

I touched Lucian's cheek with my fingers. "Remember your promise."

He nodded then turned and swam hard toward the shore. Georgina, Jasmine, and Mia followed him in.

"Ready?" I asked Ren.

He nodded.

Then we both sucked in air and dove down deep in the water. It didn't take long to spot the hydra. It was huge. At this depth, it was creepy as hell to see this big, dangerous creature just hovering ten feet below a big group of swimmers. It looked like it was having a good time knowing it could pluck anyone of them at any time.

I spotted Diego, struggling to get out from between the jaws of one of its nine heads. There was no blood, so the creature hadn't bit into him. It was just playing around, probably instructed by Poseidon to detain, but not kill anyone.

We swam toward the beast. A couple of its heads took notice of us, but it didn't look worried in the least. As we got closer, Ren started to move his hands around in front of him until he formed a small cyclone. Then he sent it spinning toward the hydra's head, the one holding Diego.

As the cyclone hit, the head opened its mouth. I swooped in and grabbed Diego by the hand and dragged him to the surface. Another few minutes and I was pretty sure he would've drowned. When we came up for air, he gasped, taking in water. As he sputtered and coughed, I slapped him on the back.

"C'mon, we need to get swimming."

While I made my first strokes, I saw in the distance Lucian and the others were almost at the shore. Revana was close, as were most of the group. I looked behind me and spotted maybe ten or so still struggling in the water. We weren't going to make the top twenty-five.

For me it didn't matter, but for Ren that meant three fails.

"Ren, you need to swim faster."

"What about you?"

"Don't worry about me. I'm good."

He nodded and dove down into the water. I knew he had the power and stamina to make it.

I kept swimming alongside Diego to make sure he didn't go under. He looked exhausted, barely able to swim. I was okay with failing this trial. It didn't matter to me.

As we kept swimming, I felt the water bubbling beneath me. I stopped and glanced around at the surface. It looked like we were floating in a pot of boiling water. It was the hydra, and it was obviously unhappy.

There was more bubbling under me, each bubble getting bigger, pushing me out of the water. Then it was like a huge wave growing underneath me, lifting me, Ren, and Diego higher and higher. I risked a peek behind me and saw the hydra emerge from the water like a volcanic eruption, rolling us on top of the wave. My stomach lurched into my throat as the wave sent us crashing into the beach.

I rolled onto my back, sputtering and coughing, and looked up as Poseidon loomed over me. His smile was broad and warm.

"You all made it. You passed the trial."

I blinked at him, shocked. "We did?" I sat up to see Lucian, Georgina, Jasmine, and Mia running down the beach toward us. I looked over at Ren, who seemed as dumfounded as I felt. Diego had yet to even register we were out of the water.

Lucian reached down for my arm and pulled me up. He hugged me. "You rolled in on the wave, beating the rest of the group."

I couldn't believe it. We'd passed, despite being almost dead last. We all shared hugs and stunned congratulations. Exhaustion started to settle on each of us. I could especially see it on Ren. I grabbed his hand and squeezed.

"Thanks for coming with me."

"You're welcome."

That night when I rolled into the dorm room intent on just unzipping my wetsuit and falling into bed, I found a small box on my bed. There was a note on top. It read: *For your bravery in the face of defeat. P.*

I opened it to find a large protein bar. Laughing, I picked it up and ate it in three bites. I was asleep by the time my head hit the pillow. And I didn't dream. I had the best sleep of my life.

In the morning, I felt invigorated. I was pumped, ready for the day. I needed that energy for Ares's trial. I braided my hair, put on shorts and a T-shirt, and figured I was ready for anything.

We gathered out on the south training field where Ares waited. Behind the God stood several warriors, including Heracles and Antiope, who was rumored to be one of the greatest female warriors to ever live.

"Today," Ares bellowed, "is about single combat.

For this trial, you may choose what kind of battle. Sword, spear, or hand to hand. Depending on what you choose will determine which great warrior you will face." He gestured to those behind him. "In the old days, we would've fought to the death, but today you will fight until your opponent says otherwise. They will be the ones who determine whether you pass or fail."

One by one, everyone picked their poison. Jasmine picked the sword, Georgina chose the spear, and Lucian picked the sword. When it became my turn, I said, "Hand to hand."

Ares smiled at that, and I started to question why and whether I'd made a bad decision. "Your opponent will be Antiope."

The warrior woman stepped forward. She was no shorter than six and a half feet. Her long, golden hair was tied back in a braid, and she wore a tank top and shorts. Her muscles rippled as she walked toward me.

Ares laughed. "Have fun, Richmond. I'll inform Chiron to expect you in the infirmary later." He stepped away from the fight area.

I didn't let his smack talk rattle me. I didn't need to beat Antiope; I just needed to get her attention, let her know that I was a worthy opponent. I was quick, I was agile, and I could take a big person down. I'd taken Heracles down a few times during training.

When we were toe to toe, I nodded to her then pulled my stance back a few steps. She had a longer arm reach than I did, and I knew if she got a proper hold on me, it would be lights out, and I'd lose the match. My best defense was a strong offense. I needed to come in quick and strike her where it counted.

As soon as she put up her hands in a defensive position, I moved in. I ducked under her right hook, landing a solid jab to her midsection. It was like punching stone and my knuckles ached. I took a few steps back again, danced around her to the right, and hit her again in the side. This time she flinched; I'd found the sweet spot.

Before I could move around her again, she spun to her right and struck me with a back hand to the face. Pain exploded across my cheek and mouth. I tasted blood. The blow had knocked me back a little, but I kept my balance and came at her again. I had to avoid getting hit in the head again. She was stronger, stronger than I was, and another blow would likely knock me on my ass. I had to be sneaky, I had to attack her in a way she'd least expect it.

As I took up my stance again, I spied a quick smile on Antiope's face. She was toying with me. I took a couple steps back, leapt into the air and spun, aiming my right foot at her face. She blocked me with her arm, then pushed, like she was swatting a fly away. I landed on my side on the ground, the impact knocking my teeth together. More blood erupted into my mouth.

I couldn't let her win. I refused to.

I flipped up back onto my feet, then moved around her to the right and hit her again in the flank. She dropped her elbow to protect that side. I moved around her and jumped onto her back. I wrapped an arm around her throat before she could get her chin down and pressed. Even a big opponent needed air.

I yanked on my arm as hard as I could, as her hands came up and tried to pull me off. I had my legs wrapped around her, my ankles locked at her navel. I was a spider clinging to its web; nothing was going to get me off. She'd have to drop onto the ground if she wanted me gone.

I could hear the cheers of my friends and peers.

"Keep at it, Blue. You got her!"

After a few more seconds, Antiope tapped my hand.

I couldn't believe it. I let her go and dropped to the ground. She turned to look at me, rubbing at her throat. A purple mark was starting to blossom there.

She offered her hand to me. I took it. "Good job. You passed this trial."

Jumping up into the air, I made a whooping sound. When I landed, Lucian was there to hug me. "You're freaking amazing, Blue." He kissed me, and it wasn't a simple peck on the lips. It was a full on proper kiss with tongue.

There were several "oooohs" and wolf whistles. Then Ares was beside us, pulling us apart.

"Let's go, lover boy, it's your turn."

"Good luck."

I watched as he walked out onto the battlefield, with a sword and his shield. His opponent was Achilles, the greatest warrior to ever live. Nerves zipped through me as he battled. But I didn't have to worry. Lucian fought like the warrior I knew he'd become.

At the end, even though he lost the battle with Achilles's blade tip pressed into his neck, Achilles told him he fought bravely and valiantly. He passed the trial.

In fact all my friends passed the trial. We only had two more trials to complete then it was over, and we'd be divided into our clans. Then the real training would start. Soon, we would all be part of the Gods' Army.

CHAPTER TWENTY-FIVE

MELANY

*E*veryone was nervous for Zeus's trial, and I didn't blame them. It wasn't going to be easy for anybody. After breakfast we were told to meet in the training facility where we did our elemental classes.

"Welcome to your trial by lightning." Zeus beamed at us, like an indulgent father. It made me want to punch him in his bearded, square jaw.

"This will be a difficult trial, and most of you will fail it." He clapped his hands together, and a boom of thunder shook the foundation of the building. The floor moved beneath our feet. Light sparked between his hands, and slowly he drew them out to create a bolt of lightning. The white glow was intense, difficult to look at.

"Each of you must grasp the bolt in both hands,

and throw it at the target. The majority of you won't even be able to hold the lightning, let alone throw it. But for those who do, you will pass this trial." He stuck the bolt into the floor.

I gaped at him. All they had to do was grab and throw it? What about holding it for two minutes while being electrocuted?

"Miss Richmond, why don't you come over here with me to observe since you already endured this task?"

I did a quick squeeze of my friends' hands before moving over to stand beside Zeus.

I held my breath as the first person stepped up to grasp the lightning.

One by one, I watched as person after person tried to pick up the bolt and hold it long enough to attempt to throw it across the room at the target. Each one failed. I grimaced every time a face contorted in pain as the electrical current zipped up their arms and burned their hands.

I watched Jasmine, Ren, and Mia all attempt and fail. My heart ached for each of them.

Then Georgina stepped up. I bit down on my lip as she leaned forward and wrapped her hands around the sizzling bolt. She winced, but she didn't drop it. In fact she looked in control. With it clutched in her hands, she turned, and with one arm, she balanced it, reared back, and tossed it across the room. She missed the target but it didn't matter. She'd done the impossible. When she turned back toward me and grinned, it was then I noticed her shoes were full of dirt.

I laughed. She was absolutely brilliant. She took her affinity to the earth and literally grounded herself. I thought maybe Zeus had noticed because his lips twitched up.

The last to go was Lucian. I figured he'd been biding his time and observing how everyone else did and figuring out an advantage.

He took in a deep breath, glancing over at me. I gave him an encouraging smile. He wrapped his hands around the lightning bolt and paused there. It looked like he was trying to acclimate himself to the electrical current shooting through his body. He then lifted the bolt, turned toward the target, and reared his hand back to throw it with everything he had. The bolt struck the target right in the bullseye.

The whole room erupted into cheers. Even Zeus clapped. But that caused the building to shake again. I ran to Lucian and hugged him. When he wrapped his arms around me, I noticed his hands weren't even red.

Because it was our last night before the final trial, Zeus let us gather in the dining hall for a couple of hours before curfew. He even allowed us a few special treats to snack on. The six of us sat together at our table and gorged on ice cream sundaes and banana splits. We talked and laughed, forgetting about what was in store for us tomorrow. Not once did we mention that it could be our last night together like this. As none of us knew what happened once we were divided into our clans. Maybe we'd never see each other again. At least not until there was a war the Gods needed us to fight.

I tried to push it from my mind and just enjoy the moment with my best friends and the boy I'd fallen in love with.

When I slept that night, my dreams were filled with darkness and shadows again. But this time, I sensed a presence in the darkness. It reached out to me, asking me for something. Asking me for permission to be with me. I didn't fear the shadows, as they'd always been kind to me, so I told the presence... *Yes.*

When I woke in the morning, I felt renewed and empowered. That feeling stayed with me as we made our way to the training field, which had been transformed into an ancient battlefield with stone walls to hide behind and trenches to jump into. The sun was bright in the sky, and it seemed to shine down on Athena as she walked out onto the field.

She wore traditional Greek robes and a gold band over her short, dark curls. Her dark skin was radiant against the white robes, and she truly looked like the Goddess she was. Ares may have been the God of War, but Athena had taught us more about the art of warfare than any other deity in the academy.

And now was our chance to show her what we'd learned. Her trial was going to be a battle, literally.

"In this trial, you will be fighting against some of the best warriors this academy has produced." She swung around and gestured to the people walking onto the field. "Heracles, Medusa, Achilles, Antiope, Helen of Troy, and Bellerophon." The six champions bowed toward us. It still unnerved me to see Medusa's hair swirl around on its own. "You will be having what you would call a game of capture the flag. The object is for your team to cross the field of battle to capture this team's flag."

I nodded. It seemed easy enough. Well, not easy, but definitely not complicated.

"Instead of paintball guns and paint pellets," she said, smiling, "you will be using bows and swords and whatever weapon you have at your disposal. Don't worry, though, those arrows are blunted, as are the swords, so you won't die on the field of battle, but you will most definitely be injured."

Great. Just what I needed. More scars.

"You will split into teams of ten and go against the champion team. If you capture their flag, you pass the trial, if they capture yours, you fail." She turned her head to look at each of us. "Just words of the wise… only two teams in seventy years have ever won."

We quickly formed a team consisting of me, Jasmine, Georgina, Mia, Lucian, Ren, Marek, Jasmine's roommate, Hella, Diego, whom Lucian had convinced to defect over to us, and a quiet girl named Rosie, who I knew was an ace with a bow. For a few of us, this trial was all or nothing. Ren, Georgina, Marek, and Diego's fates all hung on the wire. I vowed to make sure that we won this battle.

We all got outfitted with shield and weapons. I took

a bow and a quiver of blunted arrows. I was better with it than a sword or spear. Lucian took a sword, of course. Once we were ready to go, we hunkered down in our home base to discuss strategy before the horn sounded.

"How in hell are we going to beat them?" Mia shook her head, already defeated. "You heard Athena —no one wins this trial."

"We don't have to beat them," I said. "Just have to distract them long enough for someone to sneak over and grab their flag."

"At least one of them will be guarding the flag." Lucian peered over at the champions, who weren't in huddle, but just standing by their home base. I noticed a couple of them even looked bored.

I wasn't so sure of that. They were demigods. They were used to winning. For them, this was child's play. It was more of a boring task in a long list of boring tasks they'd likely done over and over again for decades. Their arrogance would play against them. Or at least, we could make it play against them.

"I think this is what we should do." I picked up a stick and started to draw in the dirt.

When the horn blew, everyone but Georgina and Marek moved out from the home base. They were going to stay behind to spring the booby trap when it was needed. The rest of us split into two groups, going opposite ways. Lucian, Ren, and Rosie came with me, and Jasmine took charge of Diego, Mia, and Hella.

My team ran to the cover of a half-formed stone

wall; some of the stones were broken, as if something chipped at them. It soon became obvious what had done the chipping. Arrows came sailing toward us. I could hear them ping off the rock. Through a tiny slit in the wall, I spotted Achilles standing on top of a slight rise, shooting at us. He didn't even have a shield. And he was smiling.

"What a dick." I shook my head. "We need to show this guy what we're made of."

"I agree." Lucian grinned at me.

"Rosie, I hear you're a great shot."

She shrugged. "I'm all right."

"Okay, on three, the three of us form a shield, and when we draw his fire, Rosie, take your shot. Aim for his legs."

She grinned.

"One, two, three…"

We ran out from the wall, Lucian, Ren, and I had our shields together, creating a wall. The sound of arrows pinging echoed around us. Crouching behind us, Rosie knocked two arrows and when I nodded, she came around the right side, fired, and then ducked back behind the shields. We heard an outraged shout.

"Bloody hell!"

I looked through the slot we'd created between shields to see Achilles with red splotches on his legs. It wasn't blood, but paint. Like paint pellets, our arrows, swords, and spears must've magically produced red paint to mimic wounds. It was perfect.

Now that we had their attention, we made a run for

the next cover, while Rosie and I fired more arrows at Achilles. He dashed from his spot on the hill. One of my arrows struck him in the ass. While we regrouped, I heard a shout from the other side of the field.

"Finally. Worthy opponents!" It was Heracles, and he sounded positively joyful.

We were almost halfway across the field. More arrows rained down on our position. Achilles had found a better spot to fire from. I spied Antiope with her spear and shield. I found a hole in the wall and fired arrows back, but Antiope easily protected herself and Achilles. We needed a huge distraction to get farther down the field.

"I'm going to create a diversion. When it happens, you three run to the next cover." After affixing my shield to my back, I rubbed my hands together, an orange glow emerging. "One, two, three!"

I leapt out from behind the wall, hands thrust out. A wall of fire erupted from my palms, and I pushed it toward Achilles and Antiope. Lucian, Ren, and Rosie ran out around the other side toward the next wall of cover. The champions were so surprised by my firewall they didn't shoot any arrows.

I felt the power of the fire diminishing. Soon, I'd be exposed in the middle of the field. I spotted a cluster of fallen logs I could hide under. With one final push of the fire, I dropped my hands, snuffing the flames, sprinted to my left, and dove for cover. A couple of arrows whizzed over my head.

Being under the logs gave me a moment of

reprieve, and I turned to look back toward our club-house. I was rewarded to see our plan had worked.

"What the hell is this?" Heracles and Bellerophon were both stuck in quick sand near our post.

I put my hand over my mouth to chuckle. Georgina and Marek had combined their earth and water affinities and produced a wonderfully thick, impassable pool of quick sand, like a moat around a castle. And now, two of the champions were stuck in it. It gave me some time to get to their fort and get the flag.

Another arrow whizzed by me. Then one hit the logs I was under. They'd found my cover. I was about to pop up to find my next cover when a spear tip broke through one of the logs and nearly struck me in the arm.

"Found you." Antiope grinned down at me. She pulled back her spear, and I rolled to the right. She narrowly missed me, and then I was up on my feet, running as fast as I could.

An arrow struck the ground a sliver away from my right foot. I didn't know where I was running to, as there wasn't any good cover on this side. But I did spy a pool of shadows undulating near an outcropping of trees. I sprinted toward it, then dove into it, hoping beyond hope I wasn't making a huge mistake. An arrow zipped by me just as I sank into the ground.

Darkness swallowed me up. It was like being in a void. My body felt floaty, like I was in a sea of salt water. Picturing their home base in my mind, I ran that way, hoping I wasn't just going deeper into the abyss with no way out. Finally, I reached my destination; the air felt lighter here, like I could easily move through it. Then I saw a pinprick of light. Eventually, that light swelled, and I stepped out of the shadow and into the field.

Medusa, who had been lounging nearby inspecting her nails, startled when she spotted me pop out of nowhere. She raised her bow, but she was too slow. I'd already knocked my arrow and sent it sailing toward her. It hit her in the chest. Red paint splattered all over her white dress.

"You bitch." She lifted her head, removed her sunglasses, and I could see her eyes start to glow.

I threw my shield over my face and made a run for their fort. As I ran, the flowers and the grass and the small bushes around me turned to stone. I nearly tripped on a petrified clutch of pansies, but I leapt over them and reached their home base. Now, I just had to clamber up to the top of their fort. But that was going to be impossible with Medusa on the rampage.

She cursed up a storm as she walked toward the fort. More things turned to stone as she neared. She was almost upon me. I risked a peek over my shield to see Lucian charging at her from behind, his sword raised.

He hit her across the back, more red splotched her dress, and she stumbled forward. I dashed up the fort steps, taking them two at a time. I reached the flagpole. With my heart nearly bursting, I grabbed that flag and tore it down.

The horn sounded.

We'd won.

I jumped up and down, waving the flag. "Wohoo!!" I looked over the side of the fort to see Lucian offering his hand to Medusa to help her up. Her eyes clamped closed, she swatted it away.

"I don't need your help, junior." She stood and put on her sunglasses. She glanced up at me. "Well played."

"Thank you," I said as sweet as cherry pie.

Down the field, my team, my friends, celebrated. And it filled me with so much happiness, tears welled in my eyes. As I looked at each of them, I realized they had become my home, and I would do anything for them.

While the other teams went through their trial, we were whisked away back to our dorms to prepare for the ceremony. I wanted to celebrate with my friends, especially with Lucian, but I was assured there would be plenty of time and opportunity later to celebrate, as there was a big feast after the official dividing of the clans.

After we had all showered, a troupe of nine women came into the dorms, carrying cases and rolling in a hanger of white and gold robes. I was dumbstruck as each of the women looked exactly alike.

"They're the muses," Georgina said.

Two of the women made a beeline toward me and Georgina. They both grinned. Even the shape of their mouths and the whiteness of their teeth were identical.

"I'm Clio, this is Thalia. We're here to make you pretty."

I looked at Georgina, who shrugged. "Okay," we said in unison.

As we were being primped and polished, painted and styled, the word came in through the dorm that none of the other teams had passed the trial. I was happy we'd passed, but it saddened me to know that possibly some of the girls would be getting the boot from the academy. I may have prayed that one of those girls was Revana, but no such luck, as I saw her running around getting ready for the ceremony.

By the time Clio and Thalia had finished with us, we were both wearing the traditional white and gold robes, our makeup was flawless, our skin was dewy and glittered with the bronzer they slathered on. My hair was twisted up into a complicated braid on my head, a gold band wrapped around like a tiara. Georgina's short hair had been slicked up and pinned. Her gold band also looked like a tiara on her head. We slid our pedicured feet into sandals, and we were ready to go.

As we filed out of the dorm to head to the stadium where I'd endured the lightning trial, we caught up with Jasmine and Mia, who both looked like Goddesses. Together, united, we walked through the academy to accept our individual fates.

There was an electric energy humming through the arena when we arrived and filed into the rows of seats. I looked across the arena to find Lucian. I saw him in the third row, and he grinned when our gazes met.

All the Gods and Goddesses walked into the arena and took up positions on the edge of the circle. Like a pie, it was split into twelve pieces. Eventually, each of us would be standing in one of those slices, relegated to that for the rest of our lives. It was overwhelming when I thought about it. I wasn't sure if I truly wanted that fate.

Zeus stepped into the middle of the raised circular platform. "Welcome, recruits. You have all accomplished an amazing feat. You have successfully endured and passed enough trials to ascend to the next level of your training."

Everyone clapped and cheered.

"Now is the moment you will be divided into your blood clan. The choices are based on the skills you've developed, the affinity to certain elements and training, and the trials you've passed. We do not make these choices lightly, and we are never wrong. The clan you are assigned to will be yours for the rest of your life."

Jasmine reached for my hand. I took it, and we squeezed each other.

"After the grand celebration tonight, you will be moving to your clan's hall. There you will have your own room and be welcomed by your other clan brothers and sisters, who have gone through the same first year training as you have. You will become a family."

I looked across the arena at Lucian. I wanted him to know how I felt about him. There might never be another chance to tell him.

"When your name is called, get up and stand side by side with your God." Zeus waved a hand toward the others. "Jasmine Walker."

I squeezed her hand.

"Ares clan."

Jasmine stood, glancing down at me. "You're my best friend, Mel. I love you."

"I love you, too." A couple of tears rolled down my cheeks. I wiped them away.

She stepped down the rows and walked out into the arena and took her place near Ares.

More people were called. Every now and then, one of my friends stood and took their place in the circle.

"Ren Nakamura."

I watched as my first friend stood up.

"Poseidon clan."

I clapped hard and cheered as he moved down to the arena. He beamed as he took his spot in the circle.

Other friends were called.

Mia went to Hera clan. Rosie joined Artemis, and Diego ended up with Dionysus.

Revana landed in Aphrodite's clan, which didn't surprise me in the least, as she was as deceptive and mean as the Goddess herself. Isobel, I heard, didn't make it through the trials, and she'd already been evacuated out of the academy.

"Georgina Stewart."

I grabbed her hand. "I love you, Gina. You're going to be amazing."

"I know." She smiled.

"Demeter clan."

She stood and took her place. I was so proud of her. She deserved her place in the pantheon.

More people were called, and then my heart leapt into my throat.

"Lucian Perro."

He stood. His gaze captured mine, and I couldn't look away from him. He was beautiful in his white robes and golden waves.

"Zeus clan."

His eyes widened. He was obviously surprised at his placing. He'd told me before that he'd expected to be in Ares's clan. Everyone cheered as he walked down into the arena and took his place next to the father of all Gods. He looked good there.

More people were called. One by one, they moved down into the circle. And then I was alone in the stands. Nerves zipped through me, and I didn't know what to do. I supposed someone had to be called last, and that someone was me.

"Melany Richmond." Zeus's voice boomed all around me. "Never in the history of this academy has one recruit ever passed all twelve trials."

That caused a ripple through everyone. Some of the Gods looked at each other, obviously not knowing that was the case.

"I am at a loss on exactly where to place you, where your skills will be most valued and nurtured."

Aphrodite spoke up. "That's not possible, Zeus. She must have cheated somewhere."

"Oh, shut up," Demeter said to the Goddess. "You always think someone is cheating because that's how you work."

As the Gods squawked and squabbled amongst themselves and my peers whispered about me, I stood and watched it all, unsure of what it all meant. Out of the corner of my eye, I saw the shadows along the stadium move. Wisps of darkness curled and snaked along the floor, then wound up the few steps to the platform. The black tendrils swirled around Hera then Artemis and Apollo. They whipped around, confusion on their faces.

Finally, the wisps swirled in the middle of the platform, making a dark tornado. Zeus took a step back, his eyes narrowing. Then the tornado just froze, the shadows evaporated, and Hades stood there, looking cool and hip in his purple suit and slicked-back, dark hair.

His appearance caused a stir, and every God gasped in shock.

Zeus pointed a finger at him. "You can't be here. It's impossible."

Smiling, Hades gave a deep bow. "It is possible, brother."

"What are you doing here? How dare you come."

Hades turned his head toward me and grinned. A shiver rushed down my back.

"I'm claiming her for my own."

Thank you for reading Demigods Academy! Don't miss YEAR TWO! We hope you enjoyed Melany's adventures and can't wait to share more with you. In the meantime, we would love to read your opinion on Amazon and Goodreads! And be sure to join our EMAIL and SMS lists below to don't miss any of our future books!

Sign Up for EMAILS at:

www.KieraLegend.com

www.ElisaSAmore.com/Vip-List

To Sign Up for SMS:

Text AMORE to (844) 339 0303

Text LEGEND to (844) 339 0303

ABOUT THE AUTHORS

Kiera Legend writes Urban Fantasy and Paranormal Romance stories that bite. She loves books, movies and Tv-Shows. Her best friends are usually vampires, witches, angels and werewolves. She never hangs out without her little dragon. She especially likes writing kick-ass heroines and strong world-buildings and is excited for all the books that are coming!

Text LEGEND to 77948 to don't miss any of them (US only) or sign up at www.kieralegend.com to get an email alert when her next book is out.

FOLLOW KIERA LEGEND:
facebook.com/groups/kieralegend
facebook.com/kieralegend
authorkieralegend@gmail.com

***

Elisa S. Amore is the number-one bestselling author of the paranormal romance saga *Touched*.

Vanity Fair Italy called her "the undisputed queen of romantic fantasy." After the success of Touched, she produced the audio version of the saga featuring Hollywood star Matt Lanter (*90210*, *Timeless*, *Star Wars*) and Disney actress Emma Galvin, narrator of *Twilight* and *Divergent*. Elisa is now a full-time writer of young adult fantasy. She's wild about pizza and also loves traveling, which she calls a source of constant inspiration. With her successful series about life and death, Heaven and Hell, she has built a loyal fanbase on social media that continues to grow, and has quickly become a favorite author for thousands of readers in the U.S.

Visit Elisa S. Amore's website and join her List of Readers at www.ElisaSAmore.com

Find Elisa S. Amore on:

- facebook.com/eli.amore
- instagram.com/eli.amore
- amazon.com/Elisa-S-Amore/e/B00J1QZYM8
- twitter.com/ElisaSAmore
- bookbub.com/authors/elisa-s-amore

Made in the USA
Middletown, DE
25 March 2023

27688718R00170